英語輕鬆學

Speak English Like a Native: Entry Level

學好 入門會話 就靠這本！

Preface 序

　　《英語輕鬆學》是一套專門訓練英文口語能力的系列書籍。包含下列四本：

1 《英語輕鬆學：學好 KK 音標就靠這本！》
2 《英語輕鬆學：學好入門會話就靠這本！》
3 《英語輕鬆學：學好初級口語就靠這本！》
4 《英語輕鬆學：學好中級口語就靠這本！》

　　我們從 KK 音標開始，幫助讀者打好發音基礎，而後三本則各自以最貼近讀者的**生活經驗**為主題架構編寫。《英語輕鬆學：學好入門會話就靠這本！》以**日常實用基礎會話**為主，《英語輕鬆學：學好初級口語就靠這本！》、《英語輕鬆學：學好中級口語就靠這本！》除了會話之外，更進階到題材新穎的**短文**，讓學習不只輕鬆，還妙趣橫生。

　　內容大題的設計則有以下特點：

1 暖身單元我們結合**聽力訓練**，以重複聆聽並且搭配關鍵字詞與簡單問題的方式訓練讀者開口說。

2 正文使用**中英對照**的方式，幫助讀者快速理解內容，其後則列出該課重點單字片語，幫助讀者記憶與運用。

3 會話單元搭配口語新技能，補充英文口語的**相關進階說法**，後再使用該課相關內容設計**聽力簡短對答**，幫助讀者同時訓練聽力及口語。

4 短文單元則搭配實用詞句，補充更多相關字詞**或文法**；並且歸納出該課的重要音標做練習並朗讀課文加強發音。最後鼓勵讀者以自己對課文的印象及該課習得的單字、用語，用**自己的話**將課文**換句話說**，測驗自身對課文及相關重點的了解程度，進而活用。

5 最後討論題目的單元，鼓勵讀者與一同學習的夥伴分享自身相關經驗。而全書所有單元皆附參考答案，提供讀者練習、對照。

　　本套書為**彩色編排**，搭配精美的圖片，讓學習賞心悅目。同時為了讓讀者能更完整且有效率地學習，除了全系列套書附贈**免費專業外師朗讀音檔**之外，更請本公司王牌講解老師之一**奚永慧**（Wesley）老師搭配 Stephen、Jennifer 老師，分別錄製講解《**英語輕鬆學：學好入門會話就靠這本！**》、《**英語輕鬆學：學好初級口語就靠這本！**》、《**英語輕鬆學：學好中級口語就靠這本！**》這三本書，歡迎讀者們上「常春藤官方網站」（ivy.com.tw）及「博客來」（books.com.tw）訂購。

　　祝大家學習成功！

Contents 目錄

Chapter 3 溝通與社交 Communicating and Socializing

Chapter 4 休閒娛樂 Leisure Activities

User's Guide 使用說明

全書朗讀
音檔下載

Lesson 01

How Are You?
你好嗎？

實用會話 Dialogue

朗讀
Lesson 01

🄰 How are you today, Linda?
🄱 I'm great! And you?
🄰 Not so good.
🄱 Oh! What's the matter?
🄰 I have a cold.

🄰 琳達，妳今天好嗎？
🄱 我很好！你呢？
🄰 不太好。
🄱 喔！發生什麼事？
🄰 我得了感冒。

掃描 QR Code 聆聽
專業外師朗讀音檔。

正文使用中英對照的
方式，幫助讀者快速
理解內容。

單字片語 Vocabulary and Phrases

CH
1
基礎會話

❶ today [təˋde] *adv.* 在今天；現今 & *n.* 今天
yesterday [ˋjɛstəde] *adv.* 在昨天 & *n.* 昨天
the day before yesterday　前天
tomorrow [təˋmɔro] *adv.* 在明天 & *n.* 明天
the day after tomorrow　後天

❷ great [gret] *a.* 極好的，很棒的
Your dress looks great!
妳的洋裝好看極了！

❸ Not so good.　不太好。(前省略主詞和 be 動詞)
Not bad.　還不錯。
(I'm) Not so good.
(我) 不太好。
(The weather is) Not bad.
(天氣) 還不錯。

❹ matter [ˋmætə] *n.* 事情，問題
What's the matter with Tom?
湯姆發生什麼事了？

❺ cold [kold] *n.* 感冒 & *a.* 冷的，冰涼的
a bad / slight cold　重 / 小感冒
The weather got colder recently. (colder 為 cold 的比較級)
天氣最近轉涼。

正文後列出該課重點
單字片語，幫助讀者
記憶與運用。

口語技能 Speaking Skills

1 問候語

◆ 表示「你好嗎？」可以這樣說：
How are you? (較正式)
How're you doing? (非正式)
How's it going? (非正式)

◆ 你可以這樣回應：
I'm fine, thank you.　我很好，謝謝你。
Not so good.　不太好。
比較
How do you do?　你 / 您好！

🔑 Notes

"How do you do?" 是兩人初次見面時，表示禮貌的問候語。雖然是問句，但意思相當於中文的「你 / 您好！」。若要回應，亦可以同樣的話回應，如：

Ⓐ How do you do, Mrs. Brown?
Ⓑ How do you do, Mr. Grant?
Ⓐ 布朗女士，您好！
Ⓑ 葛蘭特先生，您好！

2 I have a cold.　我得了感冒。

◆ 表「得」了感冒或流感應使用動詞 have，如：
have a cold　得了感冒
= catch (a) cold
have (the) flu　得了流感
= get (the) flu

接著介紹口語技能，補充英文口語的相關進階說法。

替換看看 Substitution

1 「你好嗎？」可以怎麼說：

How are you?
How are you doing?
How is it going?

2 「發生什麼事了？」可以怎麼說：

What is the matter?
What is going on?
What is wrong?
What happened?

3 「我感冒了 / 我得了感冒。」可以怎麼說：

I have a cold.
I have got a cold.
I caught a cold.

替換看看提供讀者多種說法，迅速擴充該課實用精華句。

練習 Exercises

🖊 請選出適當的字詞填入空格中。

Choose the correct word(s) to complete each sentence.

have	cold	going	matter	How

1. What's the _____ with you? You look sad.
2. _____ are you doing, Jonathan?
3. How's it _____, Maggie?
4. Do you have a _____?
5. I _____ the flu.

每課最後安排練習題，測驗自身對課文及相關重點的了解程度。

練習題解答附在每頁頁尾，供讀者作答完即時驗收。

Chapter 1

基礎會話 Basic Conversation

1

How Are You?
你好嗎？

實用會話 Dialogue

朗讀 ▶ Lesson 01

A How are you today, Linda?
B I'm great! And you?
A Not so good.
B Oh! What's the matter?
A I have a cold.

A 琳達，妳今天好嗎？
B 我很好！你呢？
A 不太好。
B 喔！發生什麼事？
A 我得了感冒。

單字片語 Vocabulary and Phrases

❶ today [təˋde] *adv.* 在今天；現今 & *n.* 今天
yesterday [ˋjɛstəˋde] *adv.* 在昨天 & *n.* 昨天
the day before yesterday　　前天
tomorrow [təˋmɔro] *adv.* 在明天 & *n.* 明天
the day after tomorrow　　後天

❷ great [ɡret] *a.* 極好的，很棒的
Your dress looks great!
妳的洋裝好看極了！

❸ Not so good.　　不太好。（前省略主詞和 be 動詞）
Not bad.　　還不錯。
(I'm) Not so good.
(我) 不太好。
(The weather is) Not bad.
(天氣) 還不錯。

❹ matter [ˋmætɚ] *n.* 事情，問題
What's the matter with Tom?
湯姆發生什麼事了？

❺ cold [kold] *n.* 感冒 & *a.* 冷的，冰涼的
a bad / slight cold　　重 / 小感冒
The weather got colder recently. (colder 為 cold 的比較級)
天氣最近轉涼。

3

口語技能 Speaking Skills

1 問候語

◆ 表示「你好嗎？」可以這樣說：
How are you? (較正式)
How're you doing? (非正式)
How's it going? (非正式)

◆ 你可以這樣回應：
I'm fine, thank you.　　我很好，謝謝你。
Not so good.　　不太好。
比較
How do you do?　　你 / 您好！

🔑 Notes

"How do you do?" 是兩人初次見面時，表示禮貌的問候語。雖然是問句，但意思相當於中文的「你 / 您好！」。若要回應，亦可以同樣的話回應，如：

A How do you do, Mrs. Brown?

B How do you do, Mr. Grant?

A 布朗女士，您好！

B 葛蘭特先生，您好！

2 I have a cold.　　我得了感冒。

◆ 表「得」了感冒或流感應使用動詞 have，如：
have a cold　　得了感冒
= catch (a) cold
have (the) flu　　得了流感
= get (the) flu

替換看看 | Substitution

CH
1
基礎會話

1 「你好嗎？」可以怎麼說：

How are you?

How are you doing?

How is it going?

2 「發生什麼事了？」可以怎麼說：

What is the matter?

What is going on?

What is wrong?

What happened?

3 「我感冒了 / 我得了感冒。」可以怎麼說：

I have a cold.

I have got a cold.

I caught a cold.

5

練習 Exercises

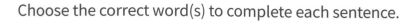

請選出適當的字詞填入空格中。

Choose the correct word(s) to complete each sentence.

have	cold	going	matter	How

1. What's the _____ with you? You look sad.
2. _____ are you doing, Jonathan?
3. How's it _____, Maggie?
4. Do you have a _____?
5. I _____ the flu.

6

Lesson 02

What's New with You?
你最近過得如何？

實用會話 Dialogue

朗讀 ▶
Lesson 02

Ⓐ Hey, Paul! What's new with you?

Ⓑ Not much. What about you?

Ⓐ I have a new boyfriend!

Ⓑ Oh! What's his name?

Ⓐ Nicholas.

Ⓐ 嘿，保羅！你最近過得如何？

Ⓑ 沒什麼特別的。妳呢？

Ⓐ 我交了新男友！

Ⓑ 喔！他叫什麼名字？

Ⓐ 尼可拉斯。

單字片語 Vocabulary and Phrases

❶ new [n(j)u] *a.* 新的，新興的；嶄新的；新來的
Nelly came up with some new ideas.
納莉想出了一些新點子。

Sarah is new to this job.
莎拉才剛開始這份工作。

❷ boyfriend [ˋbɔɪˏfrɛnd] *n.* 男朋友
girlfriend [ˋgɝlˏfrɛnd] *n.* 女朋友

❸ name [nem] *n.* 名字
first / given name　　名
last / family name　　姓氏 (= surname [ˋsɝˏnem])

My last name is Lai, and my first name is Shixiong.
我姓賴，名世雄。

口語技能 Speaking Skills

❶ 問候語

◆ 向熟識的朋友詢問「(你) 最近如何？」可以這樣說：
What's new?
What's new with you?
What's up?
How have you been?

◆ 你可以這樣回應：
a 表示「很好」：
Great!　　棒極了！
Fine! / Not bad!　　還不錯！
Everything is great / fine.　　一切都很好。
I'm doing well.　　我過得還不錯。

CH
1

基
礎
會
話

b 表示「還好」：

Not much. / Nothing much.　　沒什麼特別的。
Same as usual.　　老樣子。
I'm so-so.　　我過得馬馬虎虎 / 普普通通。
I get by.　　我還過得去。

2 What / How about you?　　那你呢？

◆ 為避免與前面提過的單字或片語重複，可用此問句作為一種簡化的表達
方式，如：
I love drinking coffee. Do you love drinking coffee, too? （可）
我愛喝咖啡。你也愛喝咖啡嗎？
→ I love drinking coffee. What / How about you? （佳）
我愛喝咖啡。那你呢？

替換看看 Substitution

1 「沒什麼特別的。」可以怎麼說：

Not much.

Nothing much.

2 「那你呢？」可以怎麼說：

What about you?

How about you?

練習 Exercises

請選出適當的字詞填入空格中。

Choose the correct word(s) to complete each sentence.

| much | about | new | name | boyfriend |

❶ I'm Gerald. What's your _____?

❷ That man over there is my _____.

❸ What's _____ with you, Allison?

❹ I'm doing really well. What _____ you?

❺ Not _____ is going on. What's up with you?

Lesson 03

Goodbye!
再見！

實用會話 Dialogue

朗讀
▶
Lesson 03

Ⓐ I have to go now. Let's talk later.
Ⓑ OK. Have a great day!
Ⓐ You, too. See you tonight.
Ⓑ Goodbye!

Ⓐ 我現在得走了。晚點再聊。
Ⓑ 好的。祝你今天順利！
Ⓐ 你也是。晚上見。
Ⓑ 再見！

單字片語 Vocabulary and Phrases

❶ now [naʊ] *adv.* & *n.* 現在，目前，此刻
right now　　現在 (= exactly now)
from now on　　從今以後

What are you doing now?
你現在在做什麼？

❷ talk [tɔk] *vi.* 談話
talk about sth　　談論某事
talk to / with sb　　和某人談話

They've been talking about the weather for half an hour.
他們已經談論天氣半小時了。

Jeffrey is talking to the manager right now.
傑佛瑞現在正在和經理談話。

❸ later [ˈletɚ] *adv.* 稍後，晚些時候
two days / weeks / months / years later　　兩天 / 週 / 個月 / 年後

❹ day [de] *n.* 一天，一日；白天
day and night　　日以繼夜

❺ tonight [təˈnaɪt] *adv.* 在今晚 & *n.* 今晚
Mark and I decided to eat out tonight.
馬克和我決定今晚外出用餐。

口語技能 Speaking Skills

❶ I have to go now.　　我現在得走了。

ⓐ have to 譯成中文為「必須」，但帶有一點勉強的意味，表示不得不做某事，或是有必要做某事。
have to V　　必須……，不得不……
I have to do the dishes tonight.
我今晚得洗碗。

b 在口語中，have to 經常被 have got to 或
gotta [ˈɡɑtə] 取代。
I have to go now.
= I've got to go now.
= I gotta go now.
　我現在得走了。

2 You, too.　　你也是。

◆ 本句中的 too 為副詞，一般使用於句尾，其前須置逗號。
too [tu] *adv.* 也，還
I like spring. Jenny does, too.
我喜歡春天。珍妮也是。

而本課會話中的 "You, too." 為一種簡答句，由 "I hope you'll have a
great day, too." (我希望你今天也過得順利。) 化簡而來。

3 道別的說法

a 一般工作或較正式的場合：
Have a great / nice / good day!　　祝你有個順利的一天！
Take care.　　保重。
Farewell.　　再見 / 再會。(較少使用)

b 一般生活或非正式的場合：
See you.　　再見。
See you later / again / soon.　　晚點見 / 改天見 / 再見。
Goodbye. / Bye.　　再見。
Catch you later.　　待會見。
Talk to you later.　　晚點 / 之後再聊。

13

替換看看 Substitution

1 「我現在得走了。」可以怎麼說：

> I have to go now.
>
> I have got to go now.
>
> I gotta go now.

2 「祝你今天順利！」可以怎麼說：

> Have a great day!
>
> Have a good day!
>
> Have a nice day!

3 「今晚 / 明天 / 晚點 / 待會 / 下次見。」可以怎麼說：

> See you tonight.
>
> See you tomorrow.
>
> See you later.
>
> See you soon.
>
> See you next time.

練習 Exercises

請選出適當的字詞填入空格中。

Choose the correct word(s) to complete each sentence.

| to | Talk | Have | too | tonight |

1 _____ to you later!

2 _____ a nice weekend, Mr. Brown!

3 I have _____ go now. It's past my bedtime.

4 See you _____ .

5 Jane likes dancing. I do, _____ .

解答 **1** Talk **2** Have **3** to **4** tonight **5** too

Lesson 04

Take Care
保重

實用會話 Dialogue

朗讀 ▶
Lesson 04

A I can't wait to see you again soon!
B Same here. I'm so happy tonight.
A Take care, Amanda.
B Bye, Marcus!

A 我等不及再見到妳了！
B 我也是。我今晚很開心。
A 亞曼達，保重。
B 馬可斯，拜拜！

單字片語 Vocabulary and Phrases

❶ can't wait to V 等不及從事……

Sophie can't wait to go to Ezra's birthday party.
蘇菲等不及要去參加埃斯拉的生日派對。

❷ wait [wet] *vi.* 等，等待
wait to V 等待從事……
wait for sb/sth 等待某人／某事

We are waiting for another chance to try again.
我們正在等待另一次嘗試的機會。

❸ again [əˈgɛn] *adv.* 又，再一次
once again 再一次（強調語氣）
all over again 重頭再來

❹ soon [sun] *adv.* 不久地，很快地

❺ Same here. 我也是。(= Me, too.)

口語技能 Speaking Skills

❶ 表達心情的說法

happy	快樂的	frustrated	沮喪的
glad	開心的	worried	擔心的
delighted	高興的	thrilled	興奮的
angry	生氣的	excited	激動的
furious	暴怒的	nervous	緊張的
sad	難過的	surprised	驚訝的

CH
1

基礎會話

I am / feel happy now.
我現在很開心。
Sally was / felt nervous during the interview.
莎莉面試時很緊張。

❷ Take care.   保重。

◆ "Take care." 原為：
Take (good) care of yourself.   （好好）照顧自己。

原意為告訴別人要保重，但實際上也常用為說再見的方式。以下其他種說法也有相似的用意：
(I wish you) All the best!   祝福你！
Stay out of trouble!   別惹麻煩！
Godspeed!   祝你好運！（較過時的說法）
Stay healthy!   保持健康！

替換看看 Substitution

❶ 「我等不及要見 / 認識你。」可以怎麼說：

I can't wait to see you.
....
I can't wait to meet you.

❷ 「我很快樂。」可以怎麼說：

I am happy.
....
I feel happy.

練習　**Exercises**

請選出適當的字詞填入空格中。

Choose the correct word(s) to complete each sentence.

feels	again	care	Take	can't

1. Vicky, I _____ wait to meet your parents!
2. Sally _____ happy because it's her birthday.
3. Please take good _____ of my pet dog.
4. I hope I can see you _____ in the future!
5. _____ care, Ben. See you next week!

Excuse Me
不好意思

實用會話 Dialogue

朗讀
Lesson 05

A Excuse me, miss. Is that your paper on the floor?
B Yes, it is. Thank you so much!
A You're welcome.

A 小姐，不好意思。掉在地上的紙是妳的嗎？
B 是的。太感謝你了！
A 不客氣。

單字片語 Vocabulary and Phrases

① **miss** [mɪs] *n.* 小姐（用以禮貌稱呼不知其名的年輕女子）

Mr. 先生（為 mister [ˋmɪstɚ] 的縮寫）

Mrs. [ˋmɪsɪz] 女士（用以禮貌稱呼已婚婦女）

Ms. [mɪz] 小姐／女士（用以稱呼婚姻狀況不明或不願提及婚姻狀況的女子）

ma'am [mæm] 女士（用以禮貌稱呼婦女）

② **paper** [ˋpepɚ] *n.* 紙（不可數）

a piece of paper 一張紙

③ **floor** [flɔr] *n.* 地板，地面

④ **You're welcome.** 不客氣。

⑤ **welcome** [ˋwɛlkəm] *a.* 受歡迎的 & *vt.* & *n.* 歡迎

give sb a warm welcome 熱烈歡迎某人

= welcome sb warmly

You are welcome to come to our house any time you want.
歡迎你隨時來我們家玩。

口語技能 Speaking Skills

① Excuse me. 不好意思／打擾一下。

◆ "Excuse me." 常用於下列時機：

ⓐ 喚起對方注意時

Excuse me. Can you give me a hand?
不好意思。你可以幫我一下嗎？

ⓑ 請對方借過時

Excuse me. Coming through.
不好意思。借過一下。

c 對於失禮行為表示歉意

Excuse me. I need to use the restroom.

不好意思。我需要上個廁所。

🔖 <u>Notes</u>

若為問句 "Excuse me?" 則可用於表示沒有聽清楚對方講的話，請對方重述。也可用於表示對於對方講的話感到冒犯而不可置信。

A I think you gained some weight.

B Excuse me? It's none of your business.

A 我覺得你胖了點。

B 你說什麼？這不關你的事。

替換看看 Substitution

1 「不好意思，小姐 / 先生 / 女士。」可以怎麼說：

> Excuse me, miss.
> ....
> Excuse me, mister.
> ....
> Excuse me, ma'am.

2 「掉在地上的紙是你的嗎？」可以怎麼說：

> Is that your paper on the floor?（floor 指室內）
> ....
> Is that your paper on the ground?（ground 指室外）

練習 Exercises

 請選出適當的字詞填入空格中。

Choose the correct word(s) to complete each sentence.

miss	Excuse	welcome	floor	paper

❶ Do you have an extra piece of _____?

❷ Ben is always _____ to our house.

❸ There is some trash on the _____.

❹ I think you dropped something, _____!

❺ _____ me, could you repeat the question?

Lesson 06

Thank You!
謝謝！

實用會話 Dialogue

朗讀 ▶
Lesson 06

A Ben, this **shirt** looks **handsome** on you.

B Thanks, Jane.

A Where is it from?

B **Actually**, it was from you!

A Oh! Now I **remember**.

A 班，你穿這件襯衫真帥氣。

B 謝啦，珍。

A 它是從哪裡來的？

B 其實，這件襯衫是妳送我的！

A 喔！現在我想起來了。

單字片語 **Vocabulary and Phrases**

❶ **shirt** [ʃɜt] *n.* 襯衫

❷ **handsome** [ˋhænsəm] *a.* 英俊的，帥氣的
= good-looking [ˌɡʊdˋlʊkɪŋ] *a.* 長相好看的

That guy over there is really handsome / good-looking.
在那裡的那位男子長得很英俊。

❸ **actually** [ˋæktʃʊəlɪ] *adv.* 事實上，實際上
= in fact

❹ **remember** [rɪˋmɛmbɚ] *vi. & vt.* 記得
I can't remember his name.
我想不起他的名字。

口語技能 **Speaking Skills**

❶ 道謝的說法

◆ Thanks (for sth).　　（為某事）謝謝。
Thank you (for sth).　　（為某事）謝謝。
Thank you so / very much.　　非常感謝。
Thanks a million.　　非常感謝。

◆ 若要回應對方的道謝，有下列幾種說法，中文均譯為「不客氣」：
You're welcome.
Don't mention it.
Not at all.
No problem.

25

2 介詞 from

◆ from 作介詞有以下幾種意思：

a 表「從……」、「來自……」（本課會話中的 from 即為此意）

Where are you from?

你來自哪裡？／你府上哪兒？

Where does this chair come from?

這張椅子是哪來的？

b 表「離……（表示距離）」

That store is a few blocks away from where we live.

那間店離我們住的地方只有幾條街而已。

c 表「從……開始（表示時間）」

The gallery is open from 9 a.m. to 6 p.m.

這間畫廊從早上九點營業至傍晚六點。

替換看看 Substitution

1 「你穿這件襯衫真帥氣／好看。」可以怎麼說：

This shirt looks handsome on you.

This shirt looks good / great / nice on you.

2 「它從哪裡來的？」可以怎麼說：

Where is it from?

Where does it come from?

練習 Exercises

請選出適當的字詞填入空格中。

Choose the correct word(s) to complete each sentence.

Thank	Thanks	remember	handsome	from

1. _____ for the gift, James. It's really nice.
2. Where is this dessert _____?
3. _____ you for your help.
4. Lily doesn't _____ my birthday.
5. You look very _____ today, David.

27

Lesson 07

Apology Accepted
我接受你的道歉

實用會話 Dialogue

朗讀 ▶ Lesson 07

A Ouch! My foot!

B I'm sorry about that.

A Apology accepted.

B Are you OK?

A Yes, I am fine. It only hurts a little.

A 哎唷！我的腳！

B 我很抱歉。

A 我接受你的道歉。

B 你還好嗎？

A 是的，我還好。有點痛
而已。

單字片語 Vocabulary and Phrases

❶ apology [əˈpɑlədʒɪ] *n.* 道歉
apologize [əˈpɑləˌdʒaɪz] *vi.* 道歉
accept one's apology / apologies　　接受某人的道歉
make an apology　　表示歉意
apologize for...　　為……道歉

❷ accept [əkˈsɛpt] *vt.* 接受
Donna is glad to accept the invite to Bruce's birthday party.
唐娜很高興地接受布魯斯生日派對的邀請。

❸ fine [faɪn] *a.* 可以接受的；好的

❹ hurt [hɜt] *vi.* 感到疼痛 & *vt.* 弄傷（三態同形）
get / be hurt　　受傷
Eric got hurt while playing soccer.
艾瑞克踢足球時受傷了。

Eric hurt his back while playing soccer.
艾瑞克踢足球時弄傷了他的背。

❺ a little　　一點，些許，稍微
= a bit
= a little bit
Can you speak a little louder, please?
= Can you speak a bit louder, please?
= Can you speak a little bit louder, please?
可以請你講話的聲音稍微大一點嗎？

口語技能 Speaking Skills

1 道歉的說法

(It's) My bad / fault / mistake. 我的錯。

(I'm) Sorry. （我）很抱歉。

I'm sorry about sth. 我為……感到抱歉。

= I'm sorry for + N/V-ing

= I'm sorry + that 子句

I apologize for + N/V-ing 我為……感到抱歉

I apologize to sb. 我向某人道歉。

I owe sb an apology. 我向某人道歉。

I'm sorry about the mess.

= I'm sorry for making a mess here.

= I'm sorry that I made a mess here.

對不起，我把這裡弄得亂七八糟。

I apologize for making a mess here.

對不起，我把這裡弄得亂七八糟。

2 回應道歉的說法

◆ 下列幾種說法，中文均譯為「沒關係」：

It's / That's OK.

It's / That's all right.

It / That doesn't matter.

No worries.

Never mind.

Apology accepted.

🔑 Notes

本段會話中的 "Apology accepted."（我原諒你。 / 我接受你的道歉。） 原應為 "Your apology is accepted by me."（你的道歉被我接受了。） 不過如此一來，整句話變得過於冗長，故外國人常以 "Apology accepted." 簡答之。

CH 1 基礎會話

替換看看 Substitution

1 「你還好嗎？」可以怎麼說：

> Are you OK?
>
> Are you fine?
>
> Are you all right?

2 「有點痛而已。」可以怎麼說：

> It only hurts a little.
>
> It only hurts a bit.
>
> It only hurts a little bit.

練習 Exercises

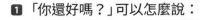 請選出適當的字詞填入空格中。

Choose the correct word(s) to complete each sentence.

little	sorry	hurt	worries	Apology

1 I'm _____ for my mistake. I won't do it again.

2 Ouch! I think I _____ my foot.

3 _____ accepted. Please be careful next time.

4 Jamie looks a(n) _____ nervous.

5 It's OK. No _____ .

解答 **1** sorry **2** hurt **3** Apology **4** little **5** worries

31

Lesson 08

Good Morning
早安

實用會話 **Dialogue**

朗讀 ▶

Lesson 08

A Good morning, Mom.
B Scott! Why aren't you at school?
A What? What day is today?
B Today is Monday!
A Oh, no!

A 媽媽，早安。
B 史考特！你怎麼沒有去學校？
A 什麼？今天是星期幾？
B 今天是星期一！
A 喔，糟了！

單字片語 | Vocabulary and Phrases

❶ morning [ˈmɔrnɪŋ] *n.* 早晨，上午
on Monday / Sunday morning　　星期一 / 日的早晨
this / yesterday / tomorrow morning　　今 / 昨 / 明天早晨
the early morning　　清晨

❷ school [skul] *n.* 學校
at school　　在學校
before / after school　　上學前 / 放學後

口語技能 | Speaking Skills

❶ Good morning.　　早安。

◆ 日常問候可以這樣說：
Good morning.　　早安。
Good afternoon.　　午安。
Good evening.　　晚安。

🔑 Notes

"Good night." 中文翻譯亦為「晚安。」，但 "Good night." 的使用時機是在晚上道別或睡覺前，並非打招呼的用語，與 "Good evening." 用意不同。

❷ 星期的說法

Monday [ˈmʌnde]	星期一
Tuesday [ˈt(j)uzde]	星期二
Wednesday [ˈwɛnzde]	星期三
Thursday [ˈθɝzde]	星期四
Friday [ˈfraɪde]	星期五
Saturday [ˈsætɚde]	星期六
Sunday [ˈsʌnde]	星期日

替換看看 Substitution

❶ 「早 / 午 / 晚安。」可以怎麼說：

Good morning.

Good afternoon.

Good evening.

❷ 「今天是星期一 / 二 / 三 / 四 / 五 / 六 / 日。」可以怎麼說：

Today / It is Monday.

Today / It is Tuesday.

Today / It is Wednesday.

Today / It is Thursday.

Today / It is Friday.

Today / It is Saturday.

Today / It is Sunday.

練習 **Exercises**

請選出適當的字詞填入空格中。

Choose the correct word(s) to complete each sentence.

school	Sunday	morning	night	on

1. What did you do _____ Monday?
2. Good _____, Andrew! How have you been?
3. Today isn't Saturday. It is _____.
4. Is Amy at _____ right now?
5. I have to go now. Good _____!

解答 1 on 2 morning 3 Sunday 4 school 5 night

Lesson 09

What Day Is Today?
今天是星期幾？

實用會話 Dialogue

朗讀 ▶
Lesson 09

Ⓐ Dear, what day is today?

Ⓑ I don't **know**, and I don't **care**.

Ⓐ Ha ha! I love **holidays**!

Ⓑ Me, too!

Ⓐ 親愛的，今天是星期幾？

Ⓑ 我不知道，也不在乎。

Ⓐ 哈哈！我愛度假！

Ⓑ 我也是！

單字片語 Vocabulary and Phrases

1 **know** [no] *vi.* & *vt.* 知道，瞭解
(三態為：know, knew [nju], known [non])

Do you know what day it is today?
你知道今天是星期幾嗎？

2 **care** [kɛr] *vi.* & *vt.* 在乎；在意
care about...　　在乎……

All parents care about their children.
所有的父母都在乎他們的小孩。

3 **holiday** [ˋhɑləˏde] *n.* 假日，假期
a national / public holiday　　國定假日

口語技能 Speaking Skills

1 What day is today?　　今天是星期幾？

◆ 本句原為 "What day is it today?"，句中的 it 是表時間的代名詞，使
用時可將 it 省略。此問句除了與時間副詞 today（今天）搭配，亦可與時
間副詞 tomorrow（明天）或 the day after tomorrow（後天）搭配，如
下：
What day is (it) today?　　今天是星期幾？
What day is (it) tomorrow?　　明天是星期幾？
What day is (it) the day after tomorrow?　　後天是星期幾？

◆ 你可以這樣回應：
It's Monday (today / tomorrow / the day after
tomorrow).
今 / 明 / 後天是星期一。
Today / Tomorrow / The day after tomorrow is Monday.
今 / 明 / 後天是星期一。

2 對等連接詞

◆ 對等連接詞有三個：

and　和
or　　或
but　　但是

這些連接詞可用來連接對等的單字、片語或子句。本課會話中的 "I don't know, and I don't care."（我不知道，我也不在乎。）即為有對等連接詞 and 連接兩個對等主要子句 "I don't know" 以及 "I don't care"。

替換看看　Substitution

1 「今 / 明 / 後天是星期幾？」可以怎麼說：

What day is (it) today?

What day is (it) tomorrow?

What day is (it) the day after tomorrow?

練習 Exercises

CH
1

基礎會話

請選出適當的字詞填入空格中。

Choose the correct word(s) to complete each sentence.

holidays	about	know	and	What

1 _____ day is today?

2 Brenda is excited about the summer _____.

3 Luke is good at math _____ science.

4 I don't _____ who Simon is.

5 I don't care _____ sports. They are boring to me.

What's the Date Today?
今天是幾月幾日？

實用會話 Dialogue

朗讀 ▶
Lesson 10

A Please sign and date the form.
B No problem. Um... What's the date today?
A It's the 7th of March.
B Hey, it's my birthday today!

A 請在表格上簽名並簽上日期。
B 沒問題。嗯……。今天是幾月幾日？
A 今天是三月七日。
B 嘿，今天是我的生日！

單字片語 Vocabulary and Phrases

1 sign [saɪn] *vt.* & *vi.* 簽名 & *n.* 標記，指示牌
a road / warning sign　　路標 / 警示牌

The superstar signed her name on her fan's notebook.
那位超級巨星在她粉絲的筆記本上簽名。
Please sign here.
請在這裡簽名。

2 date [det] *vt.* 寫上日期 & *vi.* 始於 (某時期) & *n.* 日期
The letter is dated February 21st.
這封信上寫的日期是二月二十一日。

The museum dates from the 19th century.
= The museum dates back to the 19th century.
這座博物館的歷史可追溯自十九世紀。

3 form [fɔrm] *n.* 表格
an application form　　申請表
fill in / out the form　　填寫表格

4 birthday [ˈbɝθˌde] *n.* 生日
a birthday party / cake / present　　生日派對 / 蛋糕 / 禮物

41

口語技能 Speaking Skills

1 月分的說法

January [ˈdʒænjʊˌɛrɪ]	一月	July [dʒuˈlaɪ]	七月
February [ˈfɛbruˌɛrɪ]	二月	August [ˈɔgəst]	八月
March [mɑrtʃ]	三月	September [sɛpˈtɛmbɚ]	九月
April [ˈeprəl]	四月	October [ɑkˈtobɚ]	十月
May [me]	五月	November [noˈvɛmbɚ]	十一月
June [dʒun]	六月	December [dɪˈsɛmbɚ]	十二月

2 日期的表達方式

◆ 日期有以下幾種表達方式：
月分 + 日期, 年分 (美式，常用於日常口語與書寫)
日期 + 月分(,) 年分 (英式，常用於日常書寫)
the 日期 of 月分(,) 年分 (較正式，口語與書寫上皆可使用)

◆ 根據上述，「2019 年三月七日」可以這樣表示：
March 7th, 2019
7th March(,) 2019
the 7th of March(,) 2019

3 時間副詞的用法

◆ 本課會話中的兩個句子 "What's the date today?"
（今天是幾月幾日？）以及 "It's my birthday today!"
（今天是我的生日！）皆在句尾使用了時間副詞 today。時間副詞，
如 today（今天）、yesterday（昨天）、tomorrow（明天）、next week
（下週）、this year（今年）等等，可置句首或句尾。
I have to attend a meeting <u>tomorrow</u>.（句子較短，可置句尾）
我明天得參加一場會議。
<u>Tomorrow</u> I have to attend a meeting at 3 p.m. in the meeting
room.（句子較長，可置句首）
明天我得參加一場表定下午三點於會議室舉行的會議。

替換看看 Substitution

1 「今天是三月七日。」可以怎麼說：

> It's the 7th of March (today).
>
> It's March 7th (today).

2 「今天／明天／這星期五／下星期五是我的生日！」可以怎麼說：

> It's my birthday today!
>
> It's my birthday tomorrow!
>
> It's my birthday this Friday!
>
> It's my birthday next Friday!

練習 Exercises

 請選出適當的字詞填入空格中。

Choose the correct word(s) to complete each sentence.

birthday	January	of	sign	form

❶ Please _____ your name here.

❷ You need to fill out this _____ .

❸ Today is the 21st _____ September.

❹ Today is my _____ .

❺ The first month of the year is _____ .

Lesson 11

What's Today's Date?
今天是幾月幾日？

實用會話 Dialogue

朗讀 ▶ Lesson 11

Ⓐ Jennie, this **project** is **due** on August 31st. Don't **forget**!

Ⓑ I **won't**. What's today's date?

Ⓐ Today is August 31st!

Ⓑ Oh, no!

Ⓐ 珍妮，這項計畫預計在八月三十一日完成。別忘了！

Ⓑ 我不會忘的。今天是幾月幾日？

Ⓐ 今天是八月三十一日！

Ⓑ 喔，糟了！

單字片語 Vocabulary and Phrases

❶ **project** [ˈprɑdʒɛkt] *n.* 計畫

❷ **due** [dju] *a.* 預定的；到期的

The author's latest novel is due to be released next week.
這位作家的最新小說預計在下個星期發售。

This first payment is due on April 14th.
第一期款項應在四月十四日支付。

❸ **forget** [fɚˈgɛt] *vi.* & *vt.* 忘記
（三態為：forget, forgot [fɚˈgɑt], forgotten [fɚˈgɑtn̩]）

forget to V　　忘了做……

forget + V-ing　　忘了曾做過……

I forgot to bring my keys.
我忘了帶鑰匙。

Helen forgot seeing Jack before.
海倫忘了曾經見過傑克。

❹ **I won't.**　　我不會。（won't 為 will not 的縮寫）

口語技能 Speaking Skills

❶ What's today's date?　　今天是幾月幾日？

◆ 表「日期」的英文為 date，因此詢問日期時，應使用 date，而非 day。
詢問日期有下列幾種說法：
What's the date today / tomorrow?　　今 / 明天是幾月幾日？
= What's today's / tomorrow's date?
= What date is (it) today / tomorrow?

◆ 回答有下列幾種說法：
It's April 30th (today / tomorrow).　　今 / 明天是四月三十日。
= It's the 30th of April (today / tomorrow).
= Today / Tomorrow is April 30th.

2 介詞 on 與日期並用

◆ 確切的日期與星期須與介詞 on 並用，如：

on May 2nd　　在五月二日

on Monday　　在星期一

Peter was born on May 2nd, 2016.

彼得出生於 2016 年五月二日。

That restaurant is closed on Mondays.

那間餐廳星期一休息。

🔑 **Notes**

morning（早上）、afternoon（下午）、evening（傍晚）如與日期或星期並用時，介詞亦使用 on，如：

on the afternoon of May 2nd　　在五月二日下午

on Monday morning　　在星期一早上

We went to visit the museum on the afternoon of May 2nd.

我們五月二日的下午去參觀了博物館。

What did you do on Monday morning?

你星期一早上做了什麼？

替換看看 Substitution

1 「今天是幾月幾日？」可以怎麼說：

What is the date today?

What is today's date?

What date is (it) today?

❷「這項計畫預計在八月三十一日 / 星期五 / 星期二早上完成。」
可以怎麼說：

> This project is due on August 31st.
>
> This project is due on Friday.
>
> This project is due on Tuesday morning.

練習 Exercises

請選出適當的字詞填入空格中。

Choose the correct word(s) to complete each sentence.

on	due	project	forget	date

❶ Don't _____ to bring your homework.

❷ Britney, what's the _____ today?

❸ The essay is _____ tomorrow.

❹ Daniel, did you finish your _____?

❺ Our anniversary is _____ January 15th.

解答 ❶ forget ❷ date ❸ due ❹ project ❺ on

Lesson 12

Do You Have the Time?
你知道現在幾點嗎？

實用會話 Dialogue

朗讀 ▶
Lesson 12

🅐 Pardon me. Do you have the time?

🅑 Yes. It's half past six.

🅐 Thanks a lot.

🅑 No worries.

🅐 打擾一下。你知道現在幾點嗎？

🅑 知道。現在是六點半。

🅐 多謝。

🅑 不客氣。

單字片語 Vocabulary and Phrases

❶ **Pardon me.**　打擾一下。／不好意思。
= Excuse me.

> 🔑 **Notes**
>
> Pardon (me)?　對不起，請再說一遍好嗎？
> = May I beg your pardon?
> = I beg your pardon?
> = Beg your pardon?

❷ **a lot**　非常，很大程度地
My parents used to go to Singapore a lot.
我的父母以前常去新加坡。

❸ **No worries.**　不客氣。／沒關係。
Ⓐ I'm sorry that I called you by the wrong name.
Ⓑ No worries!
Ⓐ 叫錯了你的名字，我很抱歉。
Ⓑ 沒關係！

口語技能 Speaking Skills

❶ Do you have the time?　你知道現在幾點嗎？

ⓐ 本課會話中的 "Do you have the time?" 為詢問他人時間的常見說法，不過務必要記得，在 time 前加上定冠詞 the 才是表示詢問時間，若沒有加上 the，則為詢問對方有沒有空。
Do you have the time?　你知道現在幾點嗎？
Do you have time?　你有空嗎？

ⓑ 詢問時間的其他說法：
What time is it?　現在幾點了？
What's the time?　現在幾點了？
Have you got the time?　你知道現在幾點嗎？

2 時間的說法

a 整點時，有下列幾種說法：

It's one (o'clock).　　現在是一點 (整)。

It's one a.m./p.m.　　現在是凌晨一點 / 下午一點。

📌 **Notes**

若為「中午十二點」或「午夜十二點」，除了以 o'clock 表示之外，也可以名詞 noon（中午）、midnight（午夜）表示：

It's (twelve) noon / midnight.

現在是中午 / 午夜十二點。

b 分針在一到九分時，有下列幾種說法：

It's five past three.　　現在是三點五分。

= It's three-o-five.

It's seven past nine.　　現在是九點七分。

= It's nine-o-seven.

📌 **Notes**

十分之後不可加 "o"，即：

It's three-o-eleven.（×）

→ It's three eleven.（○）

= It's eleven past three.

現在是三點十一分。

c 分針指到十五分時，有下列幾種說法：
　　It's six fifteen.　　現在是六點十五分。
= It's fifteen past six.
= It's a quarter past six.
　　＊ a quarter [ˋkwɔrtɚ] 原表示「四分之一」，即有十五分之意。

d 分針指到三十分時，有下列幾種說法：
　　It's ten thirty.　　現在是十點半。
= It's half past ten.

e 分針在三十一到五十九分時，有下列幾種說法：
　　It's fifteen to two.
= It's a quarter to two.
= It's one forty-five.
　　再過十五分鐘就兩點了。/ 現在是一點四十五分。
　　It's ten to four.
= It's three fifty.
　　再過十分鐘就四點了。/ 現在是三點五十分。

替換看看　Substitution

❶ 「打擾一下 / 不好意思。」可以怎麼說：

> Pardon me.
>
> Excuse me.

❷ 「現在幾點了？」可以怎麼說：

> Do you have the time?
>
> Have you got the time?
>
> What's the time?
>
> What time is it?

3 「現在是六點半。」可以怎麼說：

> It's half past six.
>
> It's six thirty.

練習 **Exercises**

🔑 請選出適當的字詞填入空格中。

Choose the correct word(s) to complete each sentence.

have	quarter	past	Pardon	time

1 It's a _____ to nine.

2 Do you have the _____, Mrs. Smith?

3 Excuse me, ma'am. Do you _____ the time?

4 _____ me. Where is the train station?

5 The meeting starts at half _____ nine.

Lesson 13

What Time Is It?
現在幾點？

實用會話 Dialogue

朗讀
Lesson 13

A What time is it, Michael?

B Let me check... It's 6:05 p.m.

A Oh my!

B What's wrong?

A Turn on the TV! My show is on!

A 麥可，現在幾點了？

B 讓我看看……。現在是晚上六點五分。

A 我的天哪！

B 怎麼了？

A 把電視打開！我的節目要開始了！

單字片語 Vocabulary and Phrases

1 let [lɛt] *vt.* 讓，允許 (三態同形)
I'll let you take a rest later.
我待會兒會讓你休息一下。

2 check [tʃɛk] *vi.* & *vt.* 檢查
The conductor is now checking the tickets.
列車長現在正在查票。

3 wrong [rɔŋ] *a.* 不正確的，錯誤的
right [raɪt] *a.* 正確的

4 turn on / off...   打開 / 關掉……的電源
Ella asked her sister to turn on / off the air conditioner.
艾拉請她的妹妹把冷氣打開 / 關掉。

5 show [ʃo] *n.* (電視或廣播的) 節目
a TV / radio show   電視 / 廣播節目

口語技能 Speaking Skills

1 Let me check...   讓我看看……。

◆ 顧名思義，使役動詞皆具有「使某人做某事」的意思，是口語會話中常出現的句型。常用的使役動詞有：let (讓，允許)、make (使，令)、have (叫)，本課介紹使役動詞 let 的用法，如下：

a let + 受詞 + 原形動詞
Iris let her son go picnicking.
　　　　　受詞　原形動詞
艾莉絲讓她的兒子去野餐。

b let + 受詞 + 作副詞用的介詞 (也稱為介副詞，
如 in、out、down 等)
The owner let the guest in.
　　　　　　　　　受詞　　介詞
老闆讓客人進來。

c 本課會話中的 "Let me check..." (讓我看看……。)，即在使役動詞
let 後置受詞 me (我) 以及原形動詞 check (查看)。

2 Turn on the TV!　　把電視打開！

◆ 祈使句為省略主詞，並以原形動詞起首的句子，常用在表示請求、命令
的語氣中。在口語會話中，常以較強烈的語氣表達。
Be quiet! (句首省略主詞 You，以原形 be 動詞起首)
安靜一點！

◆ 本課會話中的 "Turn on the TV!" (把電視打開！) 亦為在句首省略主詞
You，並以原形動詞 turn 起首的祈使句。

替換看看 Substitution

1 「讓我看看。」可以怎麼說：

> Let me check.
> ....
> Let me see.

2 「把電視打開 / 關掉！」可以怎麼說：

> Turn on the TV!
> ....
> Turn off the TV!

練習 Exercises

請選出適當的字詞填入空格中。

Choose the correct word(s) to complete each sentence.

Let	wrong	show	turn	What

❶ _____ time is it, Sam?

❷ Is there anything _____?

❸ Be quiet! _____ me talk!

❹ Martin asked his dad to _____ on the TV.

❺ This is my favorite TV _____.

How's the Weather over There?
那邊天氣如何？

實用會話 Dialogue

朗讀 ▶
Lesson 14

A Hello?
B Hi, Kathy. It's Mark. I'm in **London** right now!
A Wow! How's the **weather** over there?
B **Terrible**. It's **raining** cats and dogs.

A 喂？
B 凱西，妳好。我是馬克。我現在人在倫敦！
A 哇！那邊天氣如何？
B 糟透了。正在下傾盆大雨。

CH
1

基礎會話

單字片語 **Vocabulary and Phrases**

❶ London [ˈlʌndən] *n.* 倫敦（城市名）

❷ weather [ˈwɛðɚ] *n.* 天氣（不可數）

❸ terrible [ˈtɛrəbḷ] *a.* 很糟的，很差的；可怕的
You look terrible!
你臉色看起來很糟！

❹ rain [ren] *vi.* 下雨 & *n.* 雨（不可數）
be raining cats and dogs　　下傾盆大雨
= be raining hard
= be pouring

It is raining cats and dogs in Tokyo.
= It is raining hard in Tokyo.
= It is pouring in Tokyo.
東京正在下傾盆大雨。

The rain will stop soon.
雨很快就會停了。

口語技能 **Speaking Skills**

❶ I'm in London right now!　　我現在人在倫敦！

> **ⓐ** 本句中，right now 等同於 now，均可翻譯為「現在」。right now 中的
> right 為副詞，有強調的功能，即「就在現在」的意思。
> **Ⓐ** Where's Mary?
> **Ⓑ** She's at the library (right) now.
> **Ⓐ** 瑪麗在哪裡？
> **Ⓑ** 她現在在圖書館。

然而，由於現在式本身已表示「現在」，故句尾的 now 或
right now 可予以省略。即：
She's at the library (right) now.
= She's at the library.

b 根據上述，課文中的句子亦可將句尾的 right now 省略。即：
I'm in London right now!
= I'm in London now!
= I'm in London!

2 詢問天氣如何

◆ 表示「天氣如何？」有下列兩種說法：
How's (= How is) the weather?
What's (= What is) the weather like?

替換看看　Substitution

1 「我現在人在倫敦！」可以怎麼說：

> I'm in London right now!
>
> I'm in London now!

2 「今天天氣如何？」可以怎麼說：

> How's the weather today?
>
> What's the weather like today?

練習 Exercises

請選出適當的字詞填入空格中。

Choose the correct word(s) to complete each sentence.

| like | raining | right | How | terrible |

1 Adam can't come to the phone. He's busy _____ now.
2 What's the weather _____ today?
3 _____ is the weather today in your hometown?
4 You look _____. Are you feeling OK?
5 It's _____ cats and dogs right now.

Lesson 15

What's the Weather Like Today?
今天天氣如何？

實用會話 Dialogue

朗讀 ▶ Lesson 15

🅰 What's the weather like today, Mom?

🅱 It's chilly outside. You should put on a jacket before you go to school.

🅰 OK. I want to wear gloves, too.

🅰 媽，今天天氣如何？

🅱 外面有點冷。你去上學前最好穿上外套。

🅰 好。我也想戴手套。

單字片語 Vocabulary and Phrases

❶ chilly [ˈtʃɪlɪ] *a.* 冷的

❷ outside [aʊtˈsaɪd] *adv.* & *prep.* 外面

Could you wait outside?
你可以到外面等嗎？

The fans stood outside the theater waiting for the star to arrive.
粉絲們站在電影院外，等待明星來臨。

❸ jacket [ˈdʒækɪt] *n.* 外套，夾克

❹ before [brˈfɔr] *conj.* 在……之前 & *prep.* 在……以前 / 前面

Clean your room before Mom comes home.
在老媽回家之前先把房間整理好。

Review the first five lessons before the exam.
考試前要複習前五課。

❺ glove [glʌv] *n.* (一隻) 手套
a pair of gloves　　一副手套

口語技能 Speaking Skills

❶ 表達天氣的說法

sunny [ˈsʌnɪ]	晴朗的，出太陽的
rainy [ˈrenɪ]	下雨的
cloudy [ˈklaʊdɪ]	多雲的，陰天的
windy [ˈwɪndɪ]	風大的，有風的
snowy [ˈsnoɪ]	下雪的，有雪的
foggy [ˈfɑgɪ]	起霧的，有霧的
smoggy [ˈsmɑgɪ]	有霧霾的

cold [kold]	冷的
chilly ['tʃɪlɪ]	寒冷的
cool [kul]	涼的，涼爽的
pleasant ['plɛzn̩t]	舒適的，宜人的
warm [wɔrm]	溫暖的
hot [hɑt]	熱的，炎熱的

A What's the weather like today?
B It's hot and sunny.
A 今天天氣如何？
B 又熱又大晴天。

2 You should put on a jacket before you go to school.
你去上學前最好穿上外套。

put on sth / put sth on　穿上 (某衣物)；戴上 (某飾品)
Oliver put on his best suit for the event.
奧利佛為了該活動穿上他最好的西裝。
Ellie put on a pair of earrings to complete the look.
艾莉戴上一副耳環使穿搭完整。
比較
take off sth / take sth off　脫下 (某衣物)；拿掉 (某飾品)
Take off your shoes.
脫下你的鞋子。

3 I want to wear gloves, too.　我也想戴手套。

wear [wɛr] *vt.* 穿著 (衣物)；戴著 (飾品)
= be dressed in sth
= have sth on

Penny is wearing a red dress.

= Penny is dressed in a red dress.

= Penny has a red dress on.

潘妮穿著紅色洋裝。

📌 Notes

be dressed in sth 為較正式的用語，通常用於書面。而 have sth on 則為較口語的用法，語意上較 wear 更隨意。

Mr. Nelson is dressed in a white suit.

奈爾森先生身穿一套白色西裝。

Ron has a white T-shirt and a pair of shorts on.

榮恩穿著白色上衣與一條短褲。

替換看看 Substitution

❶ 「外面有點冷 / 很冷 / 很熱。」可以怎麼說：

It's chilly outside.

It's cold outside.

It's hot outside.

❷ 「我也想戴手套。」可以怎麼說：

I want to wear gloves, too.

I want to have gloves on, too.

練習 Exercises

請選出適當的字詞填入空格中。

Choose the correct word(s) to complete each sentence.

outside	Put on	chilly	before	gloves

1 It's _____ today. Let's go for hot pot!

2 Lily is wearing a pair of _____ to keep her hands warm.

3 You should check the weather _____ you go out.

4 It looks cold today. _____ a hat!

5 It's raining _____ . Let's stay at home.

Chapter 2

日常生活 Daily Life

Going to Bed
上床睡覺

實用會話 Dialogue

朗讀 ▶
Lesson 16

Ⓐ Why are you **yawning** so much? Now I feel **sleepy**, too!

Ⓑ Sorry. I'm so **tired**. I'm going to bed.

Ⓐ But it's only 7 p.m.!

Ⓑ I know. I always **stay up** too **late**.

Ⓐ You shouldn't do that.

Ⓐ 你怎麼一直在打呵欠？我現在也想睡覺了！

Ⓑ 抱歉。我好累。我要去睡覺了。

Ⓐ 可是現在才晚上七點！

Ⓑ 我知道。我總是熬夜到太晚。

Ⓐ 你不應該這樣子。

單字片語 Vocabulary and Phrases

1 yawn [jɔn] *vi.* 打呵欠

2 sleepy [ˈslipɪ] *a.* 想睡的
feel sleepy　　想睡覺

3 tired [taɪrd] *a.* 累的，疲倦的
be tired out　　累壞了
= be worn [wɔrn] out
= be exhausted [ɪgˈzɔstɪd]

Jenny looks tired. She should get some rest.
珍妮看起來很累。她應該休息一下。

After running for an hour, Tom was tired out.
= After running for an hour, Tom was worn out.
= After running for an hour, Tom was exhausted.
跑了一個小時之後，湯姆累壞了。

4 stay up　　熬夜
= sit up

David is staying up to study English.
= David is sitting up to study English.
大衛熬夜念英文。

5 late [let] *adv.* 晚；遲 & *a.* 晚的，遲到的
Zack went home late last night.
查克昨晚晚回家了。

Let's go home. It's getting late.
咱們回家吧。時候不早了。

CH 2 日常生活

口語技能 Speaking Skills

1 I'm going to bed.　　我要去睡覺了。

go to bed　　上床睡覺
get up　　起床

 Notes

wake up 表「醒來；吵醒，叫醒」。表「醒來」時，意思與 get up（起床）不同。表「吵醒」或「叫醒」時，up 可以省略。

You need to go to bed at 10 p.m.
你得在晚上十點上床睡覺。

I usually get up at 6 in the morning.
我通常早上六點起床。

Don't wake up the baby.
= Don't wake the baby.
別把小寶寶吵醒了。

替換看看 Substitution

1「我好累。」可以怎麼說：

I'm so tired.

I'm tired out.

I'm exhausted.

I'm worn out.

2「我總是熬夜到太晚。」可以怎麼說：

I always stay up too late.

I always sit up too late.

練習 Exercises

請選出適當的字詞填入空格中。

Choose the correct word(s) to complete each sentence.

stay	sleepy	yawning	late	bed

1 Come on, children. It's time to go to _____ .

2 Helen feels _____ because she woke up too early today.

3 Irene was out _____ with her friends last night.

4 It is not good for you to _____ up all night.

5 Jason is so tired. He can't stop _____ .

解答 1 bed 2 sleepy 3 late 4 stay 5 yawning

Lesson 17

Wake Up!
醒來！

實用會話 Dialogue

朗讀
▶
Lesson 17

🅐 Wake up, Peter! There's an **earthquake**!

🅑 Ah! Should we run outside? Wait... I don't feel anything.

🅐 Oh... It's really **small**. Go back to sleep.

🅑 I'm **totally awake** now.

🅐 彼得，醒一醒！有地震！

🅑 啊！我們該跑到外面嗎？等等……。我什麼都沒有感覺到。

🅐 哦 ……。地震很小。回去睡覺吧。

🅑 我現在睡意全消了。

單字片語 Vocabulary and Phrases

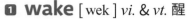

1 wake [wek] *vi.* & *vt.* 醒
（三態為：wake, woke [wok], woken [ˋwokən]）
wake up　醒過來

When do you usually wake up in the morning?
你早上通常幾點醒來？

2 earthquake [ˋɝθ͵kwek] *n.* 地震

3 small [smɔl] *a.* 小的

4 totally [ˋtotl̩ɪ] *adv.* 完全，全然
= **completely** [kəmˋplitlɪ]

5 awake [əˋwek] *a.* 清醒的 & *vi.* 醒來
（三態為：awake, awoke [əˋwok], awoken [əˋwokən]）

I was wide awake the whole night.
我整晚都沒睡。

It was raining outside when Dylan awoke.
迪倫醒來時，外頭正在下雨。

口語技能 Speaking Skills

1 Wake up, Peter!　彼得，醒一醒！

a 命令句用於請求、命令、禁止或勸告某人做某事，在口語會話中時常使用。結構上，命令句就是把主詞 You 及助動詞 must 或 should 省略了。因此，命令句的句首即為原形動詞。句尾可視該句子的語氣強弱使用驚歎號或是句號。
You must / should run!
→ Run!
跑！
You must be brave.
→ Be brave.
要勇敢。

You must / should open the window.

→ Open the window.

打開窗戶。

b 若要指定說話對象，可在命令句的前面或後面加上人名。

George, clean your room.

= Clean your room, George.

喬治，打掃你的房間。

c 命令句中也可加上 please（請），置於句首或句尾皆可。

Please take a seat.

= Take a seat, please.

請入座。

d 命令句的否定型有下列三種：

1 Don't + 原形動詞

Don't cry.

別哭。

2 Never + 原形動詞

Never talk to strangers.

千萬別跟陌生人講話。

3 No + V-ing

No smoking.

禁止抽菸。

替換看看 Substitution

1 命令句實用句：

Go back to sleep.	回去睡覺吧。
Turn on the air conditioner.	把冷氣打開。
Be on time, Frank.	要準時到，法蘭克。

2 「我現在睡意全消了。」可以怎麼說：

> I'm totally awake now.
> I'm completely awake now.
> I'm wide awake now.

練習 Exercises

請選出適當的字詞填入空格中。

Choose the correct word(s) to complete each sentence.

totally	Don't	awake	small	Wake

1 _____ up! It's time for school.
2 Jennifer is usually _____ before 7 a.m.
3 Kyle's family live in a(n) _____ town.
4 It seems Walter is _____ drunk.
5 _____ smoke! It's not healthy for you.

Lesson 18

Get out of Bed
起床

實用會話 Dialogue

朗讀 ▶
Lesson 18

Ⓐ Carrie, turn off your alarm!

Ⓑ Sorry. I didn't hear it.

Ⓐ Really? It's so loud.

Ⓑ It's not easy for me to get out of bed in the morning.

Ⓐ 凱莉,關掉妳的鬧鐘!

Ⓑ 抱歉。我沒聽到。

Ⓐ 真的嗎?它那麼大聲。

Ⓑ 早上起床對我來說很困難。

單字片語　**Vocabulary and Phrases**

❶ hear [hɪr] *vt. & vi.* 聽 (三態為：hear, heard [hɜd], heard)
You have to speak up. I can't hear you.
你說話要大聲點。我聽不到你聲音。

❷ loud [laʊd] *a.* 大聲的；吵鬧的

❸ easy [`izɪ] *a.* 簡單的，容易的

❹ morning [`mɔrnɪŋ] *n.* 早上
afternoon [͵æftə`nun] *n.* 下午
evening [`ivnɪŋ] *n.* 傍晚，晚上
in the morning / afternoon / evening　　在早上 / 下午 / 晚上

📍 Notes

因為 morning（早上）、afternoon（下午）及 evening（晚上）的時間橫跨較長，所以須與介詞 in 並用。

口語技能　**Speaking Skills**

❶ It's not easy for me to get out of bed in the morning.
早上起床對我來說很困難。

ⓐ get out of bed 即等於 get up，表「起床」。
I got out of bed / got up at 8 a.m. this morning.
我今天早上八點起床。

ⓑ get out of...　　離開……
If you can't stand the heat, get out of the kitchen.
如果你耐不住熱，就離開廚房吧 / 愛抱怨就不要做。
I need to get out of the car and stretch my legs.
我需要下車伸伸腿活動。

Notes

乘坐交通工具（如汽車或計程車等）如果不能在裡面站起來，只能坐著時，表「上車」要用 get into，表「下車」要用 get out of。但表「上／下大型交通工具（如公車、飛機、火車等）」應用 get on 或 get off。

Sandy got into a taxi at the airport.

珊蒂在機場上計程車。

Judy got out of the car for some fresh air.

茱蒂下車呼吸新鮮空氣。

Should we get on this train?

我們應該上這班火車嗎？

You should get off the bus at the next stop.

你應該在下一站下公車。

替換看看　Substitution

❶ 「早上起床對我來說很困難。」可以怎麼說：

It's not easy for me to get out of bed in the morning.

It's not easy for me to get up in the morning.

練習 Exercises

請選出適當的字詞填入空格中。

Choose the correct word(s) to complete each sentence.

hear	get out	loud	easy	get on

1 Hurry! We need to _____ this train.
2 Could you turn off the music? It's so _____.
3 Brian doesn't want to _____ of his bed yet.
4 I didn't _____ the alarm go off.
5 It is _____ for Lance to get up in the morning.

Lesson 19

Breakfast
早餐

實用會話 Dialogue

朗讀 ▶ Lesson 19

Ⓐ What do you want for breakfast?

Ⓑ I'm not hungry yet. Can you just make me a cup of black coffee?

Ⓐ Sure. Are you sure you don't want some eggs?

Ⓑ Hmm... OK. And a piece of toast!

Ⓐ 你早餐想吃什麼？

Ⓑ 我還不餓。你可以幫我弄一杯黑咖啡嗎？

Ⓐ 當然。你確定你不想要吃點蛋嗎？

Ⓑ 嗯……。好吧。加上一片吐司！

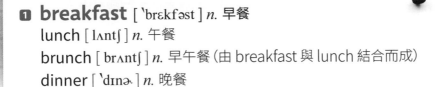

單字片語 Vocabulary and Phrases

❶ breakfast [ˈbrɛkfəst] *n.* 早餐
lunch [lʌntʃ] *n.* 午餐
brunch [brʌntʃ] *n.* 早午餐（由 breakfast 與 lunch 結合而成）
dinner [ˈdɪnɚ] *n.* 晚餐

❷ hungry [ˈhʌŋgrɪ] *a.* 餓的
I'm hungry. I need something to eat.
我餓了。我需要吃點東西。

❸ coffee [ˈkɔfɪ] *n.* 咖啡（不可數。口語上 a coffee 可表示「一杯咖啡」）
a cup of coffee　　一杯咖啡
= a coffee
two cups of coffee　　兩杯咖啡
= two coffees

❹ egg [ɛg] *n.* 蛋

❺ toast [tost] *n.* 吐司（不可數）
a piece of toast　　一片吐司
two pieces of toast　　兩片吐司

口語技能 Speaking Skills

❶ 可數名詞與不可數名詞

ⓐ 名詞可分為可數名詞與不可數名詞。可數名詞指的是可以用數字數出來的名詞，如：
an / one apple　　一顆蘋果
a / one student　　一位學生
a / one boy　　一位男孩
two apples　　兩顆蘋果
two students　　兩位學生
two boys　　兩位男孩

b 不可數名詞則為無法用數字數出來的名詞，通常為專有名詞、抽象名詞及代表物質的名詞，視為單數名詞。本課課文中的 coffee（咖啡）與 toast（吐司）即為不可數名詞。以下另舉一些常見的不可數名詞：

air [ɛr]	空氣	fruit [frut]	水果
light [laɪt]	光	meat [mit]	肉
water [ˈwɔtɚ]	水	rice [raɪs]	米飯
wind [wɪnd]	風	milk [mɪlk]	牛奶
ice [aɪs]	冰	tea [ti]	茶
wood [wʊd]	木頭	bread [brɛd]	麵包
music [ˈmjuzɪk]	音樂	paper [ˈpepɚ]	紙
money [ˈmʌnɪ]	錢	work [wɝk]	工作
food [fud]	食物	hair [hɛr]	頭髮

1 不可數名詞前面不可置不定冠詞 a 或 an，應置定冠詞 the 或所有格（my、your、his、her 等）。

The air on the mountaintop is very thin.
山頂上的空氣很稀薄。

My hair is long and dark.
我的頭髮又長、髮色又黑。

2 表示確切數量，須在不可數名詞前加上單位詞，即：

數字／不定冠詞 a(n) + 單位詞 + of + 不可數名詞

I'd like a glass of water, please.
我想要一杯水，麻煩你。

Do you have two pieces of paper?
你有兩張紙嗎？

3 表示不確切的數量，須在不可數名詞前加上 a little（一點，少許）、some（一些）、much（許多）或 a lot of（許多）。

John only has a little money.
約翰只有一點錢。

Let's listen to some music.
來聽點音樂吧。

There isn't much food left in the fridge.
冰箱裡沒剩下太多食物。
I have a lot of work to do.
我有很多工作得做。

替換看看 Substitution

1 「你早餐 / 午餐 / 晚餐想吃什麼？」可以怎麼說：

> What do you want for breakfast?
>
> What do you want for lunch?
>
> What do you want for dinner?

練習 Exercises

🖈 請選出適當的字詞填入空格中。

Choose the correct word(s) to complete each sentence.

breakfast	hungry	piece	some	cup

1 Jane drinks a _____ of coffee every morning.

2 Do you want _____ bread for breakfast?

3 The baby is crying because he's _____ .

4 I want fried eggs for _____ .

5 Cory ate a _____ of toast with his coffee.

解答 **1** cup **2** some **3** hungry **4** breakfast **5** piece

CH 2 日常生活

Having a Cup of Coffee
喝杯咖啡

實用會話 Dialogue

朗讀 Lesson 20

A One large coffee of the day, please.

B How do you take your coffee?

A One milk and one sugar.

B Here you go.

A Oh, and one vegetable sandwich.

B To stay or to go?

A To go.

A 請給我一杯大杯的每日咖啡。

B 您的咖啡想要如何調配？

A 一份牛奶與一匙糖。

B 給您。

A 喔，再加上一份蔬菜三明治。

B 內用還是外帶？

A 外帶。

單字片語 Vocabulary and Phrases

1. **large** [lɑrdʒ] *a.* 大的
   medium [ˈmidɪəm] *a.* 中的
   small [smɔl] *a.* 小的

2. **of the day** 當日的；當時的
   catch of the day 當日補獲的魚（catch 為名詞，表「漁獲量」）

3. **milk** [mɪlk] *n.* 牛奶（不可數）

4. **sugar** [ˈʃugɚ] *n.* 糖（不可數）

5. **vegetable** [ˈvɛdʒ(ə)təbl̩] *n.* 蔬菜

6. **sandwich** [ˈsændwɪtʃ] *n.* 三明治

7. **To stay or to go?** 內用還是外帶？
= For here or to go?
   to stay 內用（= for here）
   to go 外帶

口語技能 Speaking Skills

1. 與食物及飲料相關的口語慣用說法

   a / one coffee 一杯咖啡（= a / one cup of coffee）

📌 **Notes**

coffee 原為不可數名詞，應說 a / one cup of coffee 才合乎文法，但許多英語母語人士會省略 cup of，說成 a / one coffee，亦即「一杯咖啡」。

   one milk 一份牛奶

📌 **Notes**

milk 亦為不可數名詞，但和 one cup of coffee 會省略成 one coffee 一樣，有些英語母語人士在回應咖啡想要如何調配時，會說 one milk 來表達想要加一份牛奶。類似的用法亦有 cream [krim]（奶精），one cream 指「一份奶精」。

one sugar　　一匙糖

🔑 **Notes**

本文的 one sugar 原為 one spoonful of sugar（一匙糖），此處省略了 spoonful of。注意「兩匙糖」為 two spoonfuls of sugar，省略時可說 two sugars。

❷ How do you take your coffee?　　您的咖啡想要如何調配？

= How would you like your coffee?

◆ 詢問某人咖啡想要如何調配注意動詞要用 take，take 在此表「服用」。
詢問某人的食物或飲料想要如何調理，亦可使用下列句型：
How would you like your...?　　您的……想要如何調理？

🅐 How would you like your coffee?
🅑 Black with no sugar. / With sugar and cream.
🅐 您的咖啡想要如何調配？
🅑 黑咖啡不加糖。 / 加糖與奶精。

- -

🅐 How would you like your steak?
🅑 Well-done. / Medium. / Medium rare. / Rare.
🅐 您的牛排要幾分熟？
🅑 全熟。 / 五分熟。 / 三分熟。 / 一分熟。

❸ 以 here 及 there 為首的習慣用語

🅐 Here you go / are.
= There you go.
給您。 / 拿去吧。

🅐 Can I have a glass of milk?
🅑 Here you go. / Here you are. / There you go.
🅐 我可以要一杯牛奶嗎？
🅑 給您。 / 拿去吧。

b Here we are.
我們到了。

c There you go again.
你又來了。 / 你老毛病又犯了。

A Mr. Green, my dog ate my homework.
B There you go again.
A 葛林老師，我的狗把我的作業吃掉了。
B 你又來了。

替換看看　Substitution

1 「請給我一杯大杯 / 中杯 / 小杯的每日咖啡。」可以怎麼說：

> One large coffee of the day, please.
>
> One medium coffee of the day, please.
>
> One small coffee of the day, please.

2 咖啡廳點餐實用句

> One milk / cream and one sugar.　　一份牛奶 / 奶精與一匙糖。
>
> With milk / cream and sugar.　　加牛奶 / 奶精與糖。
>
> 　Double-double.　　兩份奶精與兩匙糖。
>
> = Two cream and two sugar.

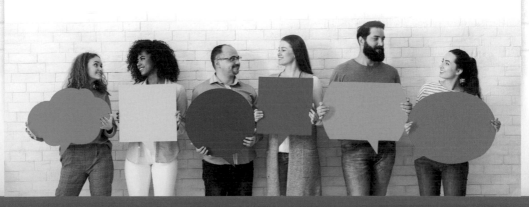

87

練習 **Exercises**

請選出適當的字詞填入空格中。

Choose the correct word(s) to complete each sentence.

takes	Here	to go	day	large

❶ Roger ordered one coffee of the _____.

❷ Your food is ready. _____ you go.

❸ The cat is drinking a _____ bowl of milk.

❹ Jamie always _____ her coffee black.

❺ One cup of hot chocolate _____, please.

解答 **❶** day **❷** Here **❸** large **❹** takes **❺** to go

Lesson 21

Running into Each Other
巧遇彼此

實用會話 Dialogue

朗
讀
▶

Lesson 21

A Wait! I can't go into this coffee shop.

B Why not?

A I might run into my ex-girlfriend. She always comes here.

B No problem. Let's go somewhere else.

A Thanks.

A 等等！我不能去這間咖啡店。

B 為什麼？

A 我可能會遇到我前女友。她都會來這間店。

B 沒問題。我們去別的地方吧。

A 謝謝。

單字片語 Vocabulary and Phrases

1 **shop** [ʃɑp] *n.* 商店

2 **run into sb** 　　與某人不期而遇

= bump into sb

On my way to work, I ran into an old friend.

= On my way to work, I bumped into an old friend.

我在上班的途中與一位老朋友不期而遇。

3 **ex-girlfriend** [ˌɛksˋgɝlfrɛnd] *n.* 前女友

ex-boyfriend [ˌɛksˋbɔɪfrɛnd] *n.* 前男友

ex-wife [ˌɛksˋwaɪf] *n.* 前妻

ex-husband [ˌɛksˋhʌzbənd] *n.* 前夫

ex- [ɛks] *prefix* 前任

ex [ɛks] *n.* 前任（可指前女友、前男友、前妻或前夫）

4 **always** [ˋɔlwez] *adv.* 總是；一直

Sam always reads books before going to bed.

山姆總會在上床睡覺前讀書。

5 **No problem.** 　　沒問題。

= No worries.

6 **somewhere** [ˋsʌmˌ(h)wɛr] *adv.* 某處

somewhere else 　　別處

I want to travel somewhere exotic.

我想去有異國風情的地方旅行。

7 **else** [ɛls] *a.* 另外的，其他的

🔑 Notes

else 常置於 some、any、no、every 為詞首的單字或疑問詞之後。

Is there something else you want to say?

你還有其他想說的嗎？

This is more important than anything else.

這比任何事情都重要。

口語技能 Speaking Skills

1 Why not?　　為什麼（不行）？

◆ "Why not?" 在口語會話中可用以表達三種意思：

a 表示贊同或同意，常譯為「有何不可？」。

Ⓐ Do you want to go to the beach with us?

Ⓑ Sure. Why not?

Ⓐ 你要跟我們一起去海灘嗎？

Ⓑ 當然。有何不可？

b 用來另提意見或建議，表示「……怎麼樣？」或「何不……？」。

Ⓐ I will start studying tomorrow.

Ⓑ Why not start studying today?

Ⓐ 我會明天開始念書。

Ⓑ 何不今天就開始念書？

c 用來詢問原因，表示「為什麼（不行）？」。

Ⓐ I can't go to the movies today.

Ⓑ Why not?

Ⓐ I have to work overtime.

Ⓐ 我今天無法去看電影。

Ⓑ 為何不行？

Ⓐ 我得加班。

CH
2

日常生活

替換看看 Substitution

1 「我可能會遇到我前女友 / 前男友 / 前夫 / 前妻。」可以怎麼說：

> I might run / bump into my ex-girlfriend.
> I might run / bump into my ex-boyfriend.
> I might run / bump into my ex-husband.
> I might run / bump into my ex-wife.

練習 Exercises

請選出適當的字詞填入空格中。

Choose the correct word(s) to complete each sentence.

else	somewhere	run	always	Why

1 _____ not go to bed early?

2 We might _____ into our friends at the theater.

3 The Wang family wants to go _____ fancy for dinner.

4 I have nothing _____ to say to you.

5 Ann and Ben _____ go out to eat for their anniversary.

Lesson 22

Dining Out
外出用餐

實用會話 Dialogue

朗
讀
▶

Lesson 22

🅐 What a delicious steak! How's your pasta?

🅑 It's not bad. Wait a minute. Eww!

🅐 What is it?

🅑 There's a long black hair in it.

🅐 How disgusting! Waiter!

🅐 真美味的牛排！你的義大利麵如何？

🅑 不差。等等。好噁心！

🅐 怎麼了？

🅑 裡面有一根長長的黑髮。

🅐 真噁心！服務生！

93

單字片語 Vocabulary and Phrases

❶ **delicious** [dɪˈlɪʃəs] *a.* 美味的

❷ **steak** [stek] *n.* 牛排

❸ **pasta** [ˈpɑstə] *n.* 義大利麵（不可數）

❹ **Wait a minute.**　　等等 / 等一下。
　　minute [ˈmɪnɪt] *n.* 分鐘

❺ **hair** [hɛr] *n.* 頭髮

> 🔖 **Notes**
>
> hair 可作可數或不可數名詞，作可數名詞時，指「一根頭髮」；作不可數名詞時，則泛指「頭髮」。

❻ **disgusting** [dɪsˈɡʌstɪŋ] *a.* 令人厭惡的
This soup tastes disgusting.
這碗湯喝起來很噁心。

❼ **waiter** [ˈwetɚ] *n.* (男) 服務生
waitress [ˈwetrɪs] *n.* 女服務生

口語技能 Speaking Skills

❶ 感歎句

◆ 本課中的 "What a delicious steak!"（真美味的牛排！）為感歎句。感歎句均由 what 或 how 引導，表示「多麼……！」或「好……！」，其句型如下：

   ⓐ What + 名詞 + 主詞 + be 動詞 / 一般動詞!
     What a good movie this is!
     真是部好電影啊！

📌 Notes

在口語會話中，通常會將句尾的「主詞 + be 動詞 / 一般動詞」予以省略，採用下列簡化的說法：

→ **What a good movie!**

　好棒的電影啊！

b How + 形容詞 / 副詞 + 主詞 + be 動詞 / 一般動詞!

How beautiful Mary is!

瑪麗好美啊！

How fast Gary runs!

蓋瑞跑得真快啊！

📌 Notes

此句型為較正式的用語，在口語上較少使用。如 what 引導的感歎句，在 how 引導的感歎句中，「主詞 + be 動詞 / 一般動詞」常予以省略，採用以下簡化的說法：

→ **How beautiful!**

　好美啊！

How fast!

好快啊！

2 詢問「怎麼了？」

◆ 詢問對方「怎麼了？」可以這樣說：

What is it? 　　怎麼了？

What's wrong? 　　怎麼了？

What's the problem? 　　有什麼問題嗎？

What's the matter? 　　有什麼問題嗎？

What happened? 　　發生什麼事了？

Is (there) something / anything wrong? 　　有什麼問題嗎？

替換看看　Substitution

1 What 引導的感歎句型實用句

> What a delicious steak!　真美味的牛排！
>
> What a polite young man (you are)!　（你）真是有禮貌的年輕人！
>
> What a cold day (it is)!　好冷的一天！

2 How 引導的感歎句型實用句

> How disgusting!　真噁心！
>
> How beautiful this view is!　真美麗的風景！
>
> How tall a tree it is!　真高的樹！

練習　Exercises

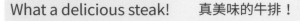 請選出適當的字詞填入空格中。

Choose the correct word(s) to complete each sentence.

How	What	minute	delicious	waiter

1 This pasta is absolutely _____!

2 Wait a _____. I left my phone at the restaurant.

3 _____ expensive this restaurant is!

4 A _____ came to take my order.

5 _____ a huge hamburger!

解答　**1** delicious **2** minute **3** How **4** waiter **5** What

Lesson 23

I'm So Full
我吃得好飽

實用會話 Dialogue

朗讀
▶
Lesson 23

Ⓐ I'm so full.

Ⓑ Me, too. What a big meal that was!

Ⓐ Now I want to see the dessert menu.

Ⓑ Are you serious?

Ⓐ Of course! This restaurant is famous for its cheesecake.

Ⓐ 我吃得好飽。

Ⓑ 我也是。那真是豐盛的一餐！

Ⓐ 我現在想看看甜點的菜單。

Ⓑ 你是認真的嗎？

Ⓐ 當然！這間餐廳就是以
它的起司蛋糕聞名。

單字片語 Vocabulary and Phrases

❶ full [fʊl] *a.* 吃飽的 (= stuffed [stʌft])；滿的

❷ meal [mil] *n.* 一餐
have a meal　　用餐

❸ dessert [dɪˋzɝt] *n.* 甜點 (不可數)
What would you like for dessert?
您甜點想要吃什麼？

❹ menu [ˋmɛnju] *n.* 菜單
Can I have the menu, please?
不好意思，我可以看一下菜單嗎？

❺ Are you serious?　　你是認真的嗎？
= Seriously?
serious [ˋsɪrɪəs] *a.* 認真的；嚴肅的；嚴重的
seriously [ˋsɪrɪəslɪ] *adv.* 認真地；嚴重地

❻ restaurant [ˋrɛstrənt / ˋrɛstərənt] *n.* 餐廳

❼ cheesecake [ˋtʃizˌkek] *n.* 起司蛋糕
a piece / slice of cheesecake　　一片起司蛋糕

口語技能 Speaking Skills

❶ What a big meal that was!　　那真是豐盛的一餐！

　◆ 本句為感歎句，可將句尾的「主詞 + be 動詞」予以省略而簡化為：
　　What a big meal that was!
　→ What a big meal!
　　真豐盛的一餐！

　◆ 本句亦可改寫為 how 引導的感歎句：
　　What a big meal that was!
　= How big a meal that was!

2 This restaurant is famous for its cheesecake.
這間餐廳就是以它的起司蛋糕聞名。

be famous [ˋfeməs] for...　因……而出名
= be famed for...
= be noted for...
= be renowned [rɪˋnaʊnd] for...
= be well-known [ˌwɛlˋnon] for...

This company	is famous for	its eco-friendly products.
	is famed for	
	is noted for	
	is renowned for	
	is well-known for	

這間公司以它環保的產品而出名。

比較

be famous as...　以……的身分聞名
= be known as...
= be renowned as...

She	is famous as	a Hollywood actress.
	is known as	
	is renowned as	

她是位著名的好萊塢女演員。

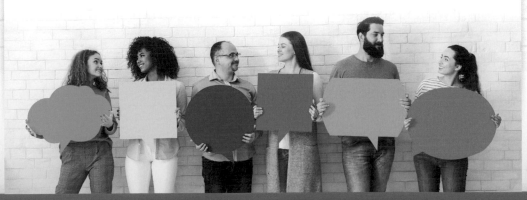

替換看看 Substitution

1 「我吃得好飽。」可以怎麼說：

> I'm so full.
>
> I'm so stuffed.

2 「這間餐廳就是以它的起司蛋糕聞名。」可以怎麼說：

> This restaurant is famous for its cheesecake.
>
> This restaurant is famed for its cheesecake.
>
> This restaurant is noted for its cheesecake.
>
> This restaurant is renowned for its cheesecake.
>
> This restaurant is well-known for its cheesecake.

練習 Exercises

請選出適當的字詞填入空格中。

Choose the correct word(s) to complete each sentence.

What	cheesecake	full	famous	menu

1 That café is _____ for its lattes.

2 I want to see the _____ . I would like to order another dish.

3 _____ a brilliant movie that was!

4 Ronnie had a piece of _____ for dessert.

5 I can't eat another bite. I'm completely _____ .

解答　**1** famous　**2** menu　**3** What　**4** cheesecake　**5** full

Talking on the Phone
講電話

實用會話 Dialogue

🅰 Hello?

🅱 Hi. May I **speak** to Emily, please?

🅰 Speaking!

🅱 Emily, this is Daniel from the **public library**. You have 10 **overdue** books. You **borrowed** them two months ago.

🅰 What?!

🅰 哈囉？

🅱 嗨。請問我可以跟艾蜜莉說話嗎？

🅰 我就是！

🅱 艾蜜莉，我是公共圖書館的 丹尼爾。妳有十本逾期未還 的書。那些書是妳在兩個月 前借的。

🅰 什麼？！

單字片語 Vocabulary and Phrases

❶ speak [spik] *vi.* 談話，交談
（三態為：speak, spoke [spok], spoken [ˈspokən]）
speak to / with sb 　和某人談話

Will is speaking to / with his client now.
威爾現在正在和他的客戶談話。

❷ public [ˈpʌblɪk] *a.* 公共的；大眾的
public transportation 　大眾運輸（系統）

❸ library [ˈlaɪˌbrɛrɪ] *n.* 圖書館

❹ overdue [ˌovəˈdju] *a.* 過期未還的；過期未付的
a day / week / month overdue 　過期一天 / 一星期 / 一個月

These library books are 5 days overdue.
這些圖書館的書逾期五天了。

❺ borrow [ˈbɑro] *vt.* (向某人) 借
borrow sth from sb 　向某人借某物

I borrowed a pen from my classmate.
我向同學借了一支筆。

口語技能 Speaking Skills

❶ 電話用語

ⓐ 來電者表明要找的對象：
May / Can / Could I speak / talk to + 人名 (, please)?
(請問) 我可以和……說話嗎？
I'd like to speak / talk to + 人名 (, please).
= I would like to speak / talk to + 人名 (, please).
我想和……說話（，麻煩你）。
Is + 人名 + there? 　……在嗎？

b 接聽者表明自己的身分：

Speaking. 我就是。

= This is he / she (speaking).

This is + 人名 (+ speaking). 我就是……。

= 人名 + speaking.

c 詢問來電者的身分：

May / Can / Could I ask who I'm speaking / talking to (, please)?

= May / Can / Could I ask who's calling (, please)?

(請問) 你 / 您是哪位呢？

d 來電者表明自己的身分：

It's + 人名 + calling. 我是……。

This is + 人名 + from + 公司名稱. 我是某公司的……。

A Hi, it's Andrew calling. May I speak to Lisa, please?

B This is she (speaking)!

A 嗨，我是安德魯。請問我可以和麗莎說話嗎？

B 我就是！

A Hello. I'd like to talk to Frank.

B Speaking. May I ask who's calling?

A This is Claire from HBB Bank.

A 哈囉。我想和法蘭克說話。

B 我就是。您是哪位呢？

A 我是 HBB 銀行的克萊兒。

替換看看 Substitution

1 「請問我可以跟艾蜜莉說話嗎？」可以怎麼說：

May I speak / talk to Emily, please?

Can I speak / talk to Emily, please?

Could I speak / talk to Emily, please?

②「我就是艾蜜莉！」可以怎麼說：

> Speaking!
>
> This is she!
>
> This is Emily!
>
> Emily speaking!

練習 Exercises

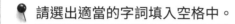 請選出適當的字詞填入空格中。

Choose the correct word(s) to complete each sentence.

May	overdue	public	borrowed	This

❶ The DVD we rented is _____ .

❷ _____ is Amy speaking. Can I ask who's calling?

❸ _____ I speak to the manager, please?

❹ The _____ library will be closed at 6 p.m. today.

❺ I _____ a few books from James last week.

 解答 ❶ overdue ❷ This ❸ May ❹ public ❺ borrowed

Lesson 25

Can I Take a Message?
我可以幫你留話嗎？

實用會話 Dialogue

朗讀 ▶
Lesson 25

🅰 Hi, Jasmine. It's Uncle Eric calling. Is your father at home?

🅱 I'm afraid not. Can I take a message?

🅰 Sure. Do you have a pen?

🅱 Yes!

🅰 OK. Tell him to give me a call at 656-8871.

🅱 Will do!

🅰 嗨，潔思敏。我是艾瑞克叔叔。
妳爸爸在家嗎？

🅱 恐怕不在。我可以幫你留話嗎？

🅰 好呀。妳有筆嗎？

🅱 有！

🅰 好的。請告訴他打 656-8871
這個號碼給我。

🅱 好的！

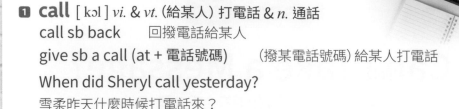

單字片語 Vocabulary and Phrases

❶ call [kɔl] *vi.* & *vt.* (給某人) 打電話 & *n.* 通話
call sb back　　回撥電話給某人
give sb a call (at + 電話號碼)　　(撥某電話號碼) 給某人打電話

When did Sheryl call yesterday?
雪柔昨天什麼時候打電話來？

I'll call Sheryl later.
= I'll give Sheryl a call later.
我待會兒會打電話給雪柔。

❷ message [ˈmɛsɪdʒ] *n.* 訊息
take a message　　(幫某人) 留言
leave a message with sb　　留言給某人轉告

❸ tell [tɛl] *vt.* 告訴，告知 (三態為：tell, told [told], told)
tell sb to V　　告知某人從事……
tell sb about sth　　告訴某人某事

Riley told me about her trip to Austria.
萊莉告訴我她的奧地利之旅。

❹ Will do!　　好的！(為口語用法，用於表示回答者將會執行被要求的事。)

口語技能 Speaking Skills

❶ Can I take a message?　　我可以幫你留話嗎？

◆ 通話時若要「替他人留話」須使用動詞 take；若要「自己留話」則須使用動詞 leave。
Can / May I take a message?　　我可以幫你留話嗎？
Can / May I leave a message?　　我可以留話嗎？

A Is Rosie there?
B She's not in. May I take a message?
A It's Jim. Tell her to call me back. Thanks.

A 蘿西在嗎？
B 她不在。我可以幫你留話嗎？
A 我是吉姆。請她回電給我。謝謝。

A Can I speak to Teresa, please?
B Sorry. She's off today.
A Oh. Can I leave a message?

A 請問我可以和泰瑞莎說話嗎？
B 抱歉。她今天請假。
A 喔。我可以留話嗎？

2 I'm afraid not. 恐怕不在。

= I'm afraid that he is not at home.

◆ 口語會話的問答中時常使用下列回應句：

I'm afraid so. 恐怕是／會。（肯定句）
I'm afraid not. 恐怕不是／不會。（否定句）

A Will it rain tomorrow?
B Yes, I'm afraid so. (so = that it will rain tomorrow)
   No, I'm afraid not. (not = that it won't rain tomorrow)

A 明天會下雨嗎？
B 是的，恐怕會下雨。
   不，恐怕不會下雨。

◆ 本課會話中的 "I'm afraid not."（恐怕不在。）即為否定句，句尾的副詞 not 等於 that he is not at home（他不在家）。

107

替換看看 Substitution

1 「恐怕他不在家。」可以怎麼說：

> I'm afraid not.
> I'm afraid that he is not at home.

2 「我可以幫你留話 / 我可以留話嗎？」可以怎麼說：

> Can I take a message?
> Can I leave a message?

3 「請告訴他打 656-8871 這個號碼給我。」可以怎麼說：

> Tell him to give me a call at 656-8871.
> Tell him to call me at 656-8871.

練習 Exercises

請選出適當的字詞填入空格中。

Choose the correct word(s) to complete each sentence.

> call   tell   give   afraid   take

1 Please _____ me more about yourself.
2 I'm _____ I can't go on the trip.
3 Please _____ me a call when you are ready.
4 May I _____ you back tomorrow?
5 Ted's not in right now. Can I _____ a message?

解答 **1** tell **2** afraid **3** give **4** call **5** take

108

Lesson 26

Sneezing and Coughing
打噴嚏與咳嗽

實用會話 Dialogue

朗讀 ▶ Lesson 26

🅐 Hi, Dr. Tyler.

🅑 Hello. What's the matter with you today, Daisy?

🅐 I've got a bad **cough** and I keep **sneezing**.

🅑 OK. I'm going to give you some **medicine**. Try to also get some **rest**. You will feel better in **a few** days.

🅐 Thank you, doctor!

🅐 泰勒醫生,您好。

🅑 哈囉。黛絲,妳今天怎麼了?

🅐 我咳得很嚴重,也一直打噴嚏。

🅑 好的。我會開一些藥給妳。也試著休息一下。幾天後妳會感覺好一點。

🅐 醫生,謝謝您!

單字片語 Vocabulary and Phrases

❶ cough [kɔf] *n.* & *vi.* 咳，咳嗽
a bad cough　　嚴重的咳嗽

❷ sneeze [sniz] *vi.* 打噴嚏 & *n.* 噴嚏 (聲)
Gary can't stop sneezing due to his allergy.
蓋瑞因為過敏所以噴嚏接連打不停。

❸ medicine [ˈmɛdəsn̩] *n.* 藥 (= medication [ˌmɛdɪˈkeʃən])；醫學
take medicine / medication　　吃 / 服藥

❹ rest [rɛst] *n.* & *vi.* 休息
take / have a rest　　休息一下

Let's take a rest before we continue the climb.
繼續爬山前我們先休息一下吧。

❺ a few　　一些，幾個
I traveled to Italy a few months ago.
我幾個月前去義大利旅行。

口語技能 Speaking Skills

❶ 與得感冒（catch a cold）有關的症狀的說法

◆ 表「有」某感冒症狀、某痛症時，應使用動詞 have，如：
have (got) a cough　　咳嗽
have (got) a sore throat　　喉嚨痛
have (got) a runny nose　　流鼻涕
have (got) a fever　　發燒
have (got) a headache / stomachache　　頭 / 肚子痛

替換看看 Substitution

1 「我咳嗽 / 喉嚨痛 / 流鼻涕 / 發燒 / 頭痛 / 肚子痛。」可以怎麼說：

I've got a cough.

I've got a sore throat.

I've got a runny nose.

I've got a fever.

I've got a headache.

I've got a stomachache.

2 「我會開一些藥給你。」可以怎麼說：

I'm going to give you some medicine.

I'm going to give you some medication.

3 「也試著休息一下。」可以怎麼說：

Try to also get some rest.

Try to also take / have a rest.

CH
2

日
常
生
活

練習 Exercises

🔖 請選出適當的字詞填入空格中。

Choose the correct word(s) to complete each sentence.

sneezing	few	medicine	cough	rest

❶ Candice will go out with a _____ friends this weekend.
❷ Rick has got a bad _____ today.
❸ I've been working nonstop. I need to get some _____.
❹ Don't forget to take your _____ with you!
❺ Linda has been _____ all day.

Lesson 27

On the Subway
地鐵上

實用會話 Dialogue

朗讀 ▶
Lesson 27

Ⓐ Miss, you can't eat or drink on the subway!

Ⓑ Really? Thanks for telling me. I'll put this hamburger and Coke away.

Ⓐ Also, that red seat is reserved for the needy.

Ⓑ Actually, I'm six months pregnant.

Ⓐ Oh, sorry!

Ⓑ Can't you see my huge belly?

Ⓐ I really can't tell!

Ⓐ 小姐,妳不能在地鐵上吃或喝東西!

Ⓑ 真的嗎?謝謝你告訴我。我會把漢堡跟可樂收起來。

Ⓐ 還有,那個紅色座位是保留給有需要的人。

Ⓑ 其實,我已經懷孕六個月了。

Ⓐ 喔,抱歉!

Ⓑ 你難道看不出來我大肚子嗎?

Ⓐ 我真的看不出來!

113

單字片語 Vocabulary and Phrases

❶ **subway** [ˋsʌbˏwe] *n.* 地鐵 (美式用法)
= underground [ˋʌndɚˏɡraʊnd] (英式用法)

❷ **hamburger** [ˋhæmbɝɡɚ] *n.* 漢堡

❸ **Coke** [kok] *n.* 可樂 (為商標，故首字應大寫)

❹ **seat** [sit] *n.* 座位 & *vt.* 使有位子坐

❺ **reserve** [rɪˋzɝv] *vt.* 保留；預訂
reserve sth for sb/sth   為某人 / 某事保留某物

This parking space is reserved for the disabled.
這個停車格是保留給身障人士的。

❻ **needy** [ˋnidɪ] *a.* 需要關懷的；貧窮的
the needy   需要關懷的人；窮人

❼ **pregnant** [ˋprɛɡnənt] *a.* 懷孕的
be pregnant with...   肚子裡懷有⋯⋯

Sarah is pregnant with her third child.
莎拉懷了第三個孩子。

❽ **huge** [hjudʒ] *a.* 巨大的，龐大的

❾ **belly** [ˋbɛlɪ] *n.* 肚子

口語技能 Speaking Skills

❶ Miss, you can't eat or drink on the subway!
小姐，妳不能在地鐵上吃或喝東西！

◆ 表「在 (大型交通工具) 上」時，介詞應使用 on，此類交通工具應為可站在
內並走動的交通工具，如 bus (公車)、train (火車)、subway (地鐵)、
plane (飛機)、ship (船) 等。
I left my jacket on the train.
我把外套忘在火車上了。

There are more than 200 people on that plane.
那架飛機上有不只兩百人。

◆ 其他只能乘坐在其中的交通工具，如 car（汽車）、
taxi（計程車）等，則應搭配介詞 in 以表示「在（交通工具）裡」。
I need to get out after sitting for so long in the car.
在車子裡坐很久之後，我需要下車。
The drunken man threw up in the taxi.
那位醉漢在計程車上吐了。

2 I'll put this hamburger and Coke away.
我會把漢堡跟可樂收起來。

put sth away / put away sth　　把某物收起來
Put your toys away before going to bed.
睡覺前把玩具都收起來。
The exam is about to start. Please put your books away.
考試即將開始。請將你們的書收起來。

比較
put sth aside / put aside sth　　把某物放在一邊；撇開某物
Roy put his work aside to help me.
羅伊把他的工作擱在一旁來幫我。
We need to put aside our differences.
我們必須撇開歧見。

替換看看 Substitution

1 「小姐，妳不能在地鐵上／在火車上／在車上吃或喝東西！」可以怎麼說：

> Miss, you can't eat or drink on the subway!
>
> Miss, you can't eat or drink on the train!
>
> Miss, you can't eat or drink in the car!

練習 Exercises

請選出適當的字詞填入空格中。

Choose the correct word(s) to complete each sentence.

reserved	Pregnant	subway	seat	needy

1 The _____ is always crowded at this time.

2 The show is about to start. Please return to your _____.

3 This parking space is _____ for the boss.

4 Only the _____ should use the elevator.

5 _____ women can get on the plane first.

解答 **1** subway **2** seat **3** reserved **4** needy **5** Pregnant

Lesson 28

On the Bus
公車上

實用會話 Dialogue

朗讀 ▶
Lesson 28

🅐 Does this bus go to the mall?

🅑 Sorry, ma'am. I only go up to 42nd Street.

🅐 So which bus should I take?

🅑 The #55 is best, but you just missed it.

🅐 Is there any other way?

🅑 I will take you to Civic Boulevard. Then you can transfer to bus #113.

🅐 Great, thanks!

🅐 這班公車會到購物中心嗎？

🅑 不好意思，女士。我只開到四十二街。

🅐 那麼我該搭哪一班公車？

🅑 55 號公車最適合，但是妳剛好錯過了。

🅐 有別的方式嗎？

🅑 我可以載妳到市民大道，然後妳可以轉搭 113 號公車。

🅐 太好了，謝謝你！

單字片語 Vocabulary and Phrases

❶ **mall** [mɔl] *n.* 購物中心

❷ **miss** [mɪs] *vt.* 錯過

Lydia missed the train and was late for work.
莉蒂亞錯過火車而上班遲到了。

❸ **way** [we] *n.* 方法，辦法；道路

Is there a way we can stop them from arguing?
我們是否有辦法可以阻止他們爭吵？

❹ **take sb to +** 地方　　帶某人去某地

Vince took me to a fancy restaurant for dinner.
文斯帶我去一間豪華餐廳吃晚餐。

❺ **civic** [ˈsɪvɪk] *a.* 市民的

❻ **boulevard** [ˈbulə͵vɑrd] *n.* 大道

❼ **transfer** [trænsˈfɝ] *vi.* & *vt.* 轉移；調動
（三態為：transfer, transferred [trænsˈfɝd], transferred）
transfer (from A) to B　　（從 A）轉移到 B

We need to transfer to another line at this station.
我們必須在這站換另一條線。

口語技能 Speaking Skills

❶ ma'am 與 sir 的用法

◆ 在路上遇到陌生人卻不知道對方的名字時，若對方為女性，可稱呼
ma'am [mæm]（為 madam [ˈmædəm] 的口語說法），表「女士」；若
對方為男性，則稱呼 sir [sɝ]，表「男士／先生」。
Do you need any help, ma'am?
妳需要幫忙嗎，女士？
Sir, could you give me a hand?
先生，你可以幫我個忙嗎？

◆ 在口語會話中，英美人士有時亦會以下列方式稱呼對方：

miss [mɪs]　　（稱呼未婚年輕女性）小姐

mister [ˋmɪstɚ]　　男士

2 I only go up to 42nd Street.　　我只開到四十二街。

go up to...　　到達……；延伸到……
This trail goes up to the lake.
這條小徑延伸到湖邊。
Our records only go up to 2010.
我們的紀錄只記到 2010 年。

比較

go up to sb　　走向某人（= walk up to sb）
Billy went / walked up to Cindy to ask her out.
比利走向辛蒂以約她出去

替換看看　Substitution

1 「不好意思，女士 / 小姐 / 先生。」可以怎麼說：

Sorry, ma'am.

Sorry, miss.

Sorry, sir.

Sorry, mister.

Lesson 28

練習 Exercises

請選出適當的字詞填入空格中。

Choose the correct word(s) to complete each sentence.

transfer	boulevard	missed	mall	ma'am

1. Excuse me, _____ . I think you're in my seat.
2. We will _____ in Boston on the way to New York.
3. Our office is located on the _____ .
4. Sally was late this morning because she _____ the bus.
5. Joy enjoys spending her weekend afternoon at the _____ .

At the Bank
在銀行

實用會話 Dialogue

朗讀 ▶
Lesson 29

A Next, please!

B Hi. I opened a **savings account** last week, but now I want to close it.

A Why is that?

B Well, I don't have much money to **save**, and I just **noticed** there's a **monthly fee**.

A Are you a student?

B Yes.

A Then you don't need to pay the fee until you **graduate**.

B Oh, great!

A 麻煩下一位！

B 嗨。我上週開了一個儲蓄帳戶，可是現在我想要關閉帳戶。

A 為什麼呢？

B 嗯，我可以存的錢不多，而且我剛注意到有月費。

A 你是學生嗎？

B 是的。

A 那直到你畢業才需要繳納費用。

B 喔，太好了！

121

單字片語 Vocabulary and Phrases

❶ next [nɛkst] *pron.* 下一位 & *a.* 下一個的

❷ savings [ˈsevɪŋz] *n.* 存款（恆為複數）

❸ account [əˈkaʊnt] *n.* 帳戶
a savings account　儲蓄帳戶

❹ save [sev] *vt.* 儲存；節省
save money / time　省錢 / 時

We traveled by plane to save time.
我們搭飛機以節省時間。

❺ notice [ˈnotɪs] *vt.* 注意到

I noticed a bruise on the little girl's arm.
我注意到那位小女孩的手臂上有瘀青。

❻ monthly [ˈmʌnθlɪ] *a.* & *adv.* 每月的 / 地
yearly [ˈjɪrlɪ] *a.* & *adv.* 每年的 / 地
weekly [ˈwiklɪ] *a.* & *adv.* 每週的 / 地
daily [ˈdelɪ] *a.* & *adv.* 每日的 / 地

The meeting is held <u>monthly</u> in our company.
= The meeting is held <u>every month</u> in our company.
= The meeting is held <u>on a monthly basis</u> in our company.
我們公司每個月舉行一次會議。

❼ fee [fi] *n.* 費用
pay a fee　付費

❽ graduate [ˈgrædʒʊˌet] *vi.* 畢業 & [ˈgrædʒʊɪt] *n.* 畢業生

口語技能 Speaking Skills

❶ 介紹常見的銀行帳戶類型

a bank account　銀行帳戶
a savings account　儲蓄 / 定存帳戶

a checking account　　支票 / 活存帳戶
a joint account　　共同帳戶

◆ 若要說「開……帳戶」，你可以這樣說：

open a... account
I wish to open a savings account, please.
我想要開個儲蓄帳戶，麻煩你。

2 介詞 until 的用法

until [ʌn'tɪl] *prep.* 直到……
= till [tɪl]
I stayed in the office until ten.
= I stayed in the office till ten.
我在辦公室待到十點。

This market is open every morning until noon.
= This market is open every morning till noon.
這個市場每天從早上營業到中午。

not... until...　　直到……才……
Penny didn't (= did not) come home until 9 o'clock.
潘妮直到九點才回到家。

You can't (= cannot) eat those oranges until they are ripe.
那些橘子熟了才能吃。

替換看看　Substitution

1 「我上週開了一個儲蓄帳戶 / 支票帳戶。」可以怎麼說：

I opened a savings account last week.

I opened a checking account last week.

2 「我剛注意到有月 / 年 / 週費。」可以怎麼說：

> I just noticed there's a monthly fee.
>
> I just noticed there's a yearly fee.
>
> I just noticed there's a weekly fee.

3 「那直到你畢業才需要繳納費用。」可以怎麼說：

> Then you don't need to pay the fee until you graduate.
>
> Then you don't need to pay the fee till you graduate.

練習 Exercises

請選出適當的字詞填入空格中。

Choose the correct word(s) to complete each sentence.

account	until	noticed	fee	monthly

1 The bank doesn't open _____ 9 a.m.

2 How much is your _____ rent for this apartment?

3 Oliver always saves his paychecks in a bank _____.

4 There's a(n) _____ if customers don't pay the bill on time.

5 Tiffany _____ that rain clouds were coming.

解答 **1** until **2** monthly **3** account **4** fee **5** noticed

Lesson 30

What Happened?
發生了什麼事？

實用會話 Dialogue

朗讀 ▶
Lesson 30

Ⓐ I need some **help** over here!

Ⓑ What **happened**?

Ⓐ The **ATM** just ate my **card**!

Ⓑ Please **describe** what happened.

Ⓐ I **put** my card **in** and **withdrew** $200. Then the **machine** said to take my card, but nothing came out.

Ⓑ Is that your card on the floor?

Ⓐ Oh! Yes, it is!

Ⓐ 我這邊需要幫忙！

Ⓑ 發生了什麼事？

Ⓐ 提款機剛剛吃了我的提款卡！

Ⓑ 請描述發生了什麼事。

Ⓐ 我把提款卡插入並領出兩百美元。然後機器說要把卡片取出，可是沒有東西跑出來。

Ⓑ 地板上的是你的提款卡嗎？

Ⓐ 喔！是的！

125

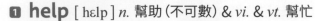

單字片語 Vocabulary and Phrases

❶ **help** [hɛlp] *n.* 幫助 (不可數) & *vi.* & *vt.* 幫忙

❷ **happen** [ˋhæpən] *vi.* 發生

Don't worry; it happens all the time.

別擔心；這件事一直都在發生。

❸ **ATM** 自動提款機 (為 automated teller machine 的縮寫)

❹ **card** [kɑrd] *n.* 卡片

an ATM card 提款卡 (美式用法)

= a cash card (英式用法)

❺ **describe** [dɪsˋkraɪb] *vt.* 描述

Can you describe the man who stole your purse?

你可以描述一下偷走你錢包的人嗎？

❻ **put sth in** 把某物放入 (put 的三態同形)

❼ **withdraw** [wɪðˋdrɔ] *vt.* 提 (款)

(三態為：withdraw, withdrew [wɪðˋdru], withdrawn [wɪðˋdrɔn])

withdraw money 提款 (= take out money)

❽ **machine** [məˋʃin] *n.* 機器

口語技能 Speaking Skills

❶ 一般過去式的使用時機

◆ 一般過去式用於表示過去的動作、習慣或狀態。使用一般過去式時，往
往會與表過去的時間副詞並用。

What did you do last night?

你昨晚做了什麼事？

I was still a student last year.

去年我還是個學生。

2 Then the machine said to take my card, ...
然後機器說要把卡片取出，……。

say to V　　說要…… (say 的三態為：say, said [sɛd], said)
= tell sb to V　　告訴某人要……
Nina said to meet her at the movie theater.
= Nina told us to meet her at the movie theater.
妮娜說在電影院跟她碰面。/ 妮娜叫我們在電影院跟她碰面。
比較
sb/sth is said to V　　據說某人 / 某事物……
Steve is said to be a rich man.
據說史蒂夫是個有錢人。

替換看看 Substitution

1 一般過去式實用句：

> The ATM just ate my card!　　提款機剛剛吃了我的提款卡！
> Tim studied for the exam all day.　　提姆整天都在為了考試苦讀。
> Sherry didn't show up at work today.　　雪莉今天沒有來上班。

2 「我把提款卡插入並領出兩百美元。」可以怎麼說：

> I put my card in and withdrew $200.
> I put my card in and took out $200.

3 「然後機器說要 / 叫我把卡片取出。」可以怎麼說：

> Then the machine said to take my card.
> Then the machine told me to take my card.

練習 Exercises

請選出適當的字詞填入空格中。

Choose the correct word(s) to complete each sentence.

| describe | card | said | helped | withdraw |

❶ Jenny wrote me a birthday _____ .

❷ I need to stop at an ATM and _____ some money.

❸ The police _____ the lost old man find his way home.

❹ Please _____ the woman you met yesterday.

❺ My boss _____ to go see him before the meeting.

Lesson 31

At the Hair Salon
在理髮廳

實用會話 Dialogue

朗讀 ▶
Lesson 31

Ⓐ Your hair feels **oily**. When was the last time that you **washed** it?

Ⓑ I just washed it last night.

Ⓐ What kind of **shampoo** did you use?

Ⓑ The **brand** is called **Silk**.

Ⓐ That one is not very good. You should try the **Royal** brand. We **sell** it here.

Ⓑ Sounds good. I'll take one **bottle**.

Ⓐ 您的頭髮摸起來很油。您上次洗頭是什麼時候？

Ⓑ 我昨晚才洗頭的。

Ⓐ 您用了哪種洗髮精？

Ⓑ 一個叫絲柔的牌子。

Ⓐ 那個牌子不太好。您應該試試看皇家牌。我們這裡有賣。

Ⓑ 聽起來不錯。我買一罐。

單字片語　Vocabulary and Phrases

❶ oily [ˋɔɪlɪ] *a.* 油膩的

❷ wash [waʃ] *vt.* 洗
Remember to wash your hands before dinner.
記得晚餐前要洗手。

❸ shampoo [ʃæmˋpu] *n.* 洗髮精 (不可數)

❹ brand [brænd] *n.* 品牌，牌子
a designer brand　　名牌

❺ silk [sɪlk] *n.* 絲
silky [ˋsɪlkɪ] *a.* 像絲一樣的

❻ royal [ˋrɔɪəl] *a.* 皇家的；皇室的
the royal family　　皇室家庭

❼ sell [sɛl] *vt.* & *vi.* 販賣，售出 (三態為：sell, sold [sold], sold)
This book sells very well.
這本書賣得很好。

❽ bottle [ˋbɑtḷ] *n.* 瓶子
a bottle of juice / shampoo　　一瓶果汁 / 一罐洗髮精

口語技能　Speaking Skills

❶ Your hair feels oily.　　您的頭髮摸起來很油。

◆ 本句中的 feel 為感官動詞，表「感覺起來 / 摸起來」。感官動詞後只能接
形容詞作主詞補語，若要加名詞則須與 like 連用，表「像……」。常見的
感官動詞有下列幾個：
feel [fil]　　感覺起來 / 摸起來
look [lʊk]　　看起來
sound [saʊnd]　　聽起來
taste [test]　　嚐起來
smell [smɛl]　　聞起來

Your skin feels so smooth.
你的皮膚摸起來很滑嫩。

Linda looks like a princess in that dress.
琳達穿那件洋裝看起來很像公主。

2 When was the last time that you washed it?
您上次洗頭是什麼時候？

last [læst] *a.* 最近的，上一次的；最後的

the last time 可表示「上一次」或「最近一次」，亦可表示「最後一次」。
The last time I saw you, you were still a baby.
我上一次見到你時，你還只是個小嬰兒。
This will be the last time that I lend you money.
這會是我最後一次借你錢。

替換看看 Substitution

1 「聽起來不錯／聽起來是個好主意。」可以怎麼說：

(It) Sounds good.
......
(It) Sounds like a good idea.

練習 **Exercises**

請選出適當的字詞填入空格中。

Choose the correct word(s) to complete each sentence.

sounds	shampoo	feel	like	smells

1 These pants _____ really comfortable.

2 It looks _____ a cold day outside.

3 The plan _____ good. What time should we meet?

4 What are you cooking? It _____ great!

5 Please wash the baby's hair with this baby _____.

 解答 **1** feel **2** like **3** sounds **4** smells **5** shampoo

Lesson 32

Cutting Hair
剪頭髮

實用會話 Dialogue

朗讀 ▶
Lesson 32

🅐 What style do you want today?

🅑 Just take a little off the sides, please.

🅐 Got it. I'm going to wash your hair first.

🅑 Sure. Mmm. That smells like vanilla.

🅐 Is the water too hot?

🅑 Nope. It's perfect. But you just splashed my eyes.

🅐 Oh, I'm sorry!

🅐 您今天想要弄什麼髮型？

🅑 兩邊剪掉一點就好，麻煩你。

🅐 知道了。我要先幫您洗頭。

🅑 好的。嗯。那個味道聞起來
很像香草。

🅐 水會太燙嗎？

🅑 不會。溫度很剛好。可是你
潑到我的眼睛了。

🅐 喔，對不起！

單字片語 Vocabulary and Phrases

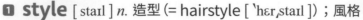

❶ **style** [staɪl] *n.* 造型 (= hairstyle [`hɛr,staɪl]) ; 風格

❷ **side** [saɪd] *n.* 側邊
the sides　　兩邊

❸ **vanilla** [və`nɪlə] *n.* 香草
vanilla ice cream　　香草冰淇淋

❹ **water** [`wɔtɚ] *n.* 水

❺ **hot** [hɑt] *a.* 熱的，燙的
cold [kold] *a.* 冷的

❻ **nope** [nop] *adv.* 不，不是 (為 no 的非正式用語)

❼ **perfect** [`pɝfɪkt] *a.* 最適當的 ; 完美的
The weather today is perfect for a picnic.
今天的天氣很適合野餐。

❽ **splash** [splæʃ] *vt.* 潑，濺
John splashed cold water on his face to wake himself up.
約翰往自己臉上潑冷水好讓自己清醒。

口語技能 Speaking Skills

❶ 有關「剪髮」的說法

◆ 表示「剪掉……」本文中使用 take，除此之外亦可用下列動詞：
cut [kʌt] *vt.* 剪 (三態同形)
trim [trɪm] *vt.* 修剪 (三態為：trim, trimmed [trɪmd], trimmed)
cut / trim sth off　　剪掉某物

◆ 根據上述，本文句子亦可改寫為：
Just take a little off the sides, please.
= Just cut a little off the sides, please.
= Just trim a little off the sides, please.
兩邊剪掉一點就好，麻煩你。

2 表示「知道了」、「明白了」的說法

◆ 表示「知道了」、「明白了」可用下列說法：

(I) Got it.　　　知道了。

I see (what you mean).　　我懂(你的意思)了。/ 原來如此。

I understand (what you mean).　　我了解(你的意思)了。

= Understood.

＊ understand [ˌʌndɚˋstænd] vt. 了解，知道

（三態為：understand, understood [ˌʌndɚˋstʊd], understood）

🔑 **Notes**

不宜說 "I know."。雖然中文翻譯亦為「我知道了。」，但語氣上帶有「我早就知道了。」的意味，並非謙虛的說法。

替換看看 **Substitution**

1 「您今天想要弄什麼髮型？」可以怎麼說：

What style do you want today?
....
What hairstyle do you want today?

2 「水會太燙 / 冷嗎？」可以怎麼說：

Is the water too hot?
....
Is the water too cold?

練習 Exercises

請選出適當的字詞填入空格中。

Choose the correct word(s) to complete each sentence.

style	vanilla	perfect	splashed	cut

1. I had my hair _____ short.
2. The naughty boy _____ water all over his mother.
3. My favorite flavor of ice cream is _____.
4. What _____ do you prefer?
5. The pants are a _____ fit.

Chapter 3

溝通與社交
Communicating and Socializing

I'm Really Sorry
我真的很抱歉

實用會話 Dialogue

朗讀 ▶
Lesson 33

Ⓐ You are 20 minutes late for work!

Ⓑ I'm really sorry, Mr. Lin.

Ⓐ This is the third time. You are fired!

Ⓐ 你工作遲到二十分鐘了！

Ⓑ 林先生，我真的很抱歉。

Ⓐ 這已經是第三次了。你被開除了！

單字片語 Vocabulary and Phrases

1 minute [ˈmɪnɪt] *n.* 分鐘

2 late [let] *a.* 遲的，晚的
five minutes / hours late   晚五分鐘 / 小時
late for work / school   上班 / 學遲到

3 work [wɜk] *n.* 工作（不可數）
比較
job [dʒɑb] *n.* 工作（可數）
be out of work / a job   失業

4 time [taɪm] *n.* 次（數），回
the first / second / next / last time   第一 / 第二 / 下 / 最後一次

Harry goes to the library three times a week.
哈利一週去圖書館三次。

This is my first time to see the snow.
這是我第一次看見雪。

5 fire [faɪr] *vt.* 開除 & *n.* 火
fire sb from sth   某人被開除某工作
fire sb for sth   因某事開除某人

John was fired from his job last week.
上星期約翰被開除了。

Meryl was fired for her dishonesty.
梅洛兒因不誠實而被開除了。

口語技能 Speaking Skills

1 I'm really sorry.　　我真的很抱歉。

◆ 要強調「非常，真的」，除了用副詞 really 之外，也可使用下列
副詞來表示：
very [ˋvɛrɪ]
awfully [ˋɔflɪ]
terribly [ˋtɛrəbl̩ɪ]
extremely [ɪkˋstriml̩ɪ]
It's awfully cold today. Let's turn on the heater.
今天真的好冷喔。我們來開暖氣吧。

2 序數詞

序數詞是表示次序 (如：第一、第二、第三……) 的數詞。

1st	first	第一	11th	eleventh	第十一
2nd	second	第二	12th	twelfth	第十二
3rd	third	第三	13th	thirteenth	第十三
4th	fourth	第四	14th	fourteenth	第十四
5th	fifth	第五	15th	fifteenth	第十五
6th	sixth	第六	20th	twentieth	第二十
7th	seventh	第七	30th	thirtieth	第三十
8th	eighth	第八	40th	fortieth	第四十
9th	ninth	第九	50th	fiftieth	第五十
10th	tenth	第十	100th	(one) hundredth	第一百

Ⓐ Which one do you want?
Ⓑ I'd like the second one.
Ⓐ 你想要哪一個？
Ⓑ 我想要第二個。

3 被動語態

◆ 英文中的語態有兩種，一種為主動，另一種則為
被動。被動語態主要將受詞當作主詞，之後置 be 動詞，
再置動詞的過去分詞。

The boss fired you.（主動）　老闆把你開除了。
　主詞　　　　受詞

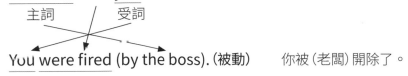

You were fired (by the boss).（被動）　你被（老闆）開除了。

替換看看　Substitution

1「我真的很抱歉。」可以怎麼說：

I'm really sorry.

I'm very sorry.

I'm awfully sorry.

I'm terribly sorry.

I'm extremely sorry.

2「這是第一／第二／第三／第四／最後一次了。」可以怎麼說：

This is the first time.

This is the second time.

This is the third time.

This is the fourth time.

This is the last time.

練習 Exercises

請選出適當的字詞填入空格中。

Choose the correct word(s) to complete each sentence.

fired	minutes	second	late	really

1 I'm _____ sorry about this.

2 This is the _____ time you hurt me!

3 Sarah waited 30 _____ for her friend.

4 Jim was _____ for stealing things from the office.

5 Ben, why are you _____ for school again?

Good Night!
晚安！

實用會話 Dialogue

Ⓐ I'm setting my alarm for 5:30 tomorrow morning.

Ⓑ Oh! Why so early?

Ⓐ I'm meeting my boss to discuss something.

Ⓑ Then let's switch off the light. It's getting late.

Ⓐ OK. Good night!

Ⓑ Night!

Ⓐ 我將明早的鬧鐘調到五點半。

Ⓑ 喔！為什麼這麼早？

Ⓐ 我要跟老闆會面討論事情。

Ⓑ 那麼關燈吧。時候不早了。

Ⓐ 好的。晚安！

Ⓑ 晚安！

單字片語 Vocabulary and Phrases

❶ set [sɛt] *vt.* 設定 (三態同形)

Remember to set the TV to record the show.
記得要設定電視錄下那個節目。

❷ alarm [əˋlɑrm] *n.* 鬧鐘；警報器
an alarm clock　　鬧鐘

❸ early [ˋɝlɪ] *a.* 早的 & *adv.* 提早

This band was famous in the early 1960s.
這個樂團在一九六〇年代初期很有名。

I have to get up early tomorrow for a meeting.
我明天要早起去參加會議。

❹ meet [mit] *vt.* & *vi.* 會面 (三態為：meet, met [mɛt], met)

I'm meeting my friends at the café.
我要去咖啡廳與朋友碰面。

When shall we meet?
我們要幾點見面？

❺ boss [bɔs] *n.* 老闆；上司

❻ switch [swɪtʃ] **off...**　　關掉……
= turn off...
　switch on...　　打開……
= turn on...

Please switch off the light. It's too bright.
= Please turn off the light. It's too bright.
請把燈關掉。它太亮了。

Sam always switches on the radio once he gets home.
= Sam always turns on the radio once he gets home.
山姆總是一回家就打開收音機。

❼ light [laɪt] *n.* 電燈 (可數)；光 (不可數)

The street lights are now on.
街燈現在亮了。

口語技能 `Speaking Skills`

❶ I'm meeting my boss to discuss something.
我要跟老闆會面討論事情。

= I'm meeting my boss to talk about something.
= I'm going to meet my boss to talk about something.

ⓐ 現在進行式除了表示「在現在的時刻，某動作正在進行」的狀態，也可用以表示即將發生的動作，此時 be 動詞（am、is、are）可譯成「即將」，且可改寫為簡單未來式。簡單未來式的句型如下：
主詞 + will + V　　將要……
= 主詞 + 現在式 be 動詞（am、is、are）+ going to + V
John is coming today.
= John will come today.
= John is going to come today.
約翰今天會來。

ⓑ discuss [drˈskʌs] *vt.* 討論
= talk about sth　　討論某事
We need to discuss the homework.
= We need to talk about the homework.
我們需要討論該作業。

❷ Then let's switch off the light.　　那麼關燈吧。

◆ 副詞 then 在口語會話中常表「那麼」。可用於會話開頭，作為交談或某行動的開始；或用於會話結尾，表示談話結束，事情已商定。
Now then, what's the plan for today?
那麼，今天的行程是什麼？

CH 3 溝通與社交

That's settled then. It's a pleasure doing business
with you.
那就這麼決定了。很榮幸與您做生意。

3 Good night!　　晚安！

◆ 表示「晚安」有許多說法。最常見的為 "Good night."。以下為其他睡前
道「晚安」的常見說法：
Good night!　　晚安！
Night!　　晚安！
Sleep tight!　　一夜好眠！
Sleep well!　　一夜好眠！
Sweet dreams!　　祝你有個美夢！

替換看看　Substitution

1 「我要跟老闆會面討論事情。」可以怎麼說：

I'm meeting my boss to discuss something.

I'm meeting my boss to talk about something.

2 「那麼關燈吧。」可以怎麼說：

Then let's switch off the light.

Then let's turn off the light.

練習 **Exercises**

📌 請選出適當的字詞填入空格中。

Choose the correct word(s) to complete each sentence.

alarm	night	switch	discuss	early

1. Good _____ . See you in the morning!
2. It's healthy to get up _____ in the morning.
3. Don't forget to set your _____ !
4. My boss wants to have a meeting to _____ the project.
5. Could you help me _____ off the light?

CH
3
溝通與社交

Long Time No See
好久不見

實用會話 Dialogue

朗讀 ▶
Lesson 35

🅐 Dan, is that you?

🅑 Lisa! Long time no see!

🅐 Yes! How are things?

🅑 Great! Let's get together sometime.

🅐 Sure. How about lunch next Monday?

🅑 Sounds like a plan!

🅐 丹，是你嗎？

🅑 麗莎！好久不見！

🅐 對啊！你過得如何？

🅑 很好！找時間聚一聚吧。

🅐 當然。下星期一吃午餐如何？

🅑 聽起來不錯！

單字片語 Vocabulary and Phrases

❶ get together　　相聚；會面
get-together [ˈɡɛttəˌɡɛðɚ] *n.* 聚會 (= gathering [ˈɡæðərɪŋ])
together [təˈɡɛðɚ] *adv.* 一起；共同

We still sometimes get together after all these years.
過了這些年後，我們有時還會聚在一起。

Wendy is hosting a small get-together at her house tonight.
溫蒂今晚要在她家辦一個小型的聚會。

❷ sometime [ˈsʌmˌtaɪm] *adv.* 某時

🔖 **Notes**

sometime 表「不知何時」，之後亦可接確切的時間如 yesterday（昨天）、tomorrow（明天）、in 2010（在2010 年）、early this morning（今早）等。

John will arrive sometime next week.
約翰下週某個時候會抵達。

I saw Tina sometime yesterday.
我昨天某個時間有見到蒂娜。

❸ How about...?　　那……如何？
= What about...?

🔖 **Notes**

此句型為一種簡化的句型，省略了重複的字詞或片語。這種句型在口語會話中很常見。

We're going home. How about you?
= We're going home. What about you?
我們要回家了。那你呢？

4 **next** [nɛkst] *a.* 下一個的；接下來的
next week / month / year　　下週 / 下個月 / 明年

🔑 **Notes**

沒有 next day 的說法，若表示「明天」應說 tomorrow [təˋmɔro]；若表示「（某一天的）隔天」則要說 the next day。

5 **Sounds like a plan!**　　聽起來不錯！
= Sounds great!
plan [plæn] *n.* 計畫

口語技能 Speaking Skills

1 Long time no see!　　好久不見！

◆ 本文的 "Long time no see!"（好久不見！）並不符合文法，但已廣為英語母語人士所接受。若表達「好久不見」時欲使用合乎文法的句子，可以這樣說：
(I) Haven't seen you for a long time!
= It's (= It has) been a long time!
= It's (= It has) been a while!

2 How are things?　　你過得如何？

= How are things with you?

◆ 本問候語原為 "How are things with you?"，句末的 with you 可省略，即成本課的 "How are things?"。問候語亦有下列常見的說法：
How are you?　　你好嗎？（多用於正式場合）
How are you doing? / How're you doing?　　你好嗎？
How have you been?　　你最近還好嗎？
How's it going?　　最近如何？
What's up?　　最近如何？（多為年輕人使用）

What's happening?　　最近如何？（多為年輕人使用）

How are you getting along?　　你好嗎？

＊ get along　　進展

替換看看 **Substitution**

1 「下星期一吃午餐如何？」可以怎麼說：

> How about lunch next Monday?
> ....
> What about lunch next Monday?

練習 **Exercises**

🔑 請選出適當的字詞填入空格中。

Choose the correct word(s) to complete each sentence.

plan	sometime	time	about	next

1 Let's get together _____ for a talk.

2 Do you want to have lunch together _____ week?

3 I'm doing fine. How _____ you?

4 Going to the beach sounds like a great _____!

5 Hey, Paul. Long _____ no see!

Lesson 36

Introducing Others
介紹他人

實用會話 Dialogue

朗讀 ▶ Lesson 36

A Wendy, come meet my **father**.

B Hi, Wendy.

C Hi. It's great to **finally** meet you, Mr. Thompson!

B What do you mean "finally?"

C Josh, doesn't your father know we are getting **married**?

A 溫蒂，來見見我爸。

B 溫蒂，妳好。

C 您好。湯普森先生，很高興終於能與您見面！

B 妳說「終於」是什麼意思？

C 喬許，你爸爸難道不知道我們要結婚了嗎？

單字片語 Vocabulary and Phrases

❶ father [ˋfɑðɚ] *n.* 父親
mother [ˋmʌðɚ] *n.* 母親

❷ finally [ˋfaɪn̩lɪ] *adv.* 終於；最後
David's dream finally came true.
大衛的夢想終於成真了。

❸ marry [ˋmærɪ] *vi.* 結婚 & *vt.* 娶；嫁
(三態為：marry, married [ˋmærɪd], married)
get married　　結婚

Chris and Becky got married on a lovely Sunday by the beach.
在一個宜人的週日，克里斯與貝琪在海灘上結婚了。

Will you marry me?
你願意嫁給我嗎？

Rumor has it that Gary is going to marry a rich widow.
謠傳蓋瑞要迎娶一位有錢的寡婦。

CH
3

溝通與社交

口語技能 Speaking Skills

❶ Josh, doesn't your father know we are getting married?
喬許，你爸爸難道不知道我們要結婚了嗎？

◆ 一般問句若以否定形態起首，可翻譯為「難道不……嗎？」。答案若為肯
定，以 Yes 回答；若為否定，則以 No 回答。
Ⓐ Isn't she beautiful?
Ⓑ Yes, she is.
Ⓐ 她難道不美嗎？
Ⓑ 不，她很美。

A Doesn't Josh live here?

B No, he doesn't.

A 喬許難道不住在這嗎？

B 對，他不住在這。

A Won't Bill join us for dinner?

B Yes, he will.

A 比爾難道不會與我們共進晚餐嗎？

B 不，他會與我們共進晚餐。

替換看看 Substitution

1 「溫蒂，來見見我爸／媽。」可以怎麼說：

Wendy, come meet my father.

Wendy, come meet my mother.

2 一般問句以否定形態起首的實用句

Josh, doesn't your father know we are getting married?
喬許，你爸爸難道不知道我們要結婚了嗎？

Can't you go to work by yourself?　你難道不能自己去上班嗎？

Isn't she your ex-girlfriend?　她難道不是你的前女友嗎？

練習 Exercises

請選出適當的字詞填入空格中。

Choose the correct word(s) to complete each sentence.

| finally | Isn't | Don't | married | father |

❶ My _____ is my role model.

❷ It's nice to _____ meet you, Debra.

❸ Jim and his girlfriend are getting _____.

❹ _____ you know who that man is?

❺ _____ today Carol's birthday?

It's a Pleasure to Meet You
很榮幸與您見面

實用會話 Dialogue

朗讀 ▶ Lesson 37

A Mrs. Sanders, this is my husband, Danny. Danny, meet my manager, Mrs. Sanders.

B It's a pleasure to meet you, Mrs. Sanders.

C Wow, he's not only handsome but also polite!

A 山德斯夫人,這是我的丈夫丹尼。丹尼,來見見我的經理,山德斯夫人。

B 山德斯夫人,很榮幸與您見面。

C 哇,他不僅長得帥氣,也很有禮貌!

單字片語 Vocabulary and Phrases

❶ husband [ˋhʌzbənd] *n.* 丈夫
  wife [waɪf] *n.* 妻子

❷ manager [ˋmænɪdʒɚ] *n.* 經理
  general manager   總經理
  assistant manager   副理

❸ pleasure [ˋplɛʒɚ] *n.* 榮幸；快樂
  It is a pleasure to + V   很榮幸……
  = It is a pleasure + V-ing
  take pleasure in + N/V-ing   樂於……，以……為樂

  It was a pleasure working with you.
  很榮幸與您合作。

  Stan takes pleasure in teasing his little sister.
  史丹很愛逗弄他的妹妹。

❹ handsome [ˋhænsəm] *a.* 帥氣的，英俊的

  Bruce is a handsome fellow.
  布魯斯是位英俊的男子。

❺ polite [pəˋlaɪt] *a.* 有禮貌的
  impolite [͵ɪmpəˋlaɪt] *a.* 無禮的

  I like John because he is polite.
  我喜歡約翰因為他很有禮貌。

  Jeff's impolite behavior made the teacher very angry.
  傑夫無禮的行為使老師非常生氣。

口語技能 Speaking Skills

❶ 介紹他人

◆ 將某人介紹給其他人認識時，要以 This is 作為開頭，
  表示「站在我旁邊的這位是……」。
  注意不應以 He 或 She 來稱呼。

Ⓐ Hey, Sally. This is Jack.

Ⓑ Hi, Jack. Nice to meet you.

Ⓐ 嘿，莎莉。這位是傑克。

Ⓑ 嗨，傑克。很高興認識你。

❷ It's a pleasure to meet you.　　很榮幸與您見面。

◆ 初次與他人見面時，欲表示「很榮幸與你見面。」或「很高興認識你。」除
了本文的 "It's a pleasure to meet you." 亦可使用下列說法：
Pleased to meet you.
Nice to meet you.
Glad to meet you.

❸ Wow, he's not only handsome but also polite!
哇，他不僅長得帥氣，也很有禮貌！

not only... but (also)...　　不僅……而且……
= not only... but... as well
＊ as well　　也；還有

📌 Notes

本片語連接詞可用以連接對等的單字、片語和子句。

　　Alice is not only lovely but also friendly.
　　　　　　　　形容詞　　　　　形容詞

= Alice is not only lovely but friendly as well.
愛麗絲不但漂亮，為人也很友善。

根據上述，本課句子可改寫如下：

　　Wow, he's not only handsome but also polite!

= Wow, he's not only handsome but polite as well!
哇，他不僅長得帥氣，也很有禮貌！

替換看看 Substitution

1 "This is..." 的實用句

Mrs. Sanders, this is my husband, Danny.
山德斯夫人，這是我的丈夫丹尼。

Amy, this is my best friend, Sam.　　艾咪，這位是我的摯友山姆。

This is Olivia. She is my coworker.
這位是奧麗薇雅。她是我的同事。

2 「很榮幸與您見面 / 很高興認識您，山德斯夫人。」可以怎麼說：

It's a pleasure to meet you, Mrs. Sanders.

Pleased to meet you, Mrs. Sanders.

Nice to meet you, Mrs. Sanders.

Glad to meet you, Mrs. Sanders.

3 "not only... but also... / not only... but... as well" 的實用句

Wow, he's not only handsome but also polite!
哇，他不僅長得帥氣，也很有禮貌！

Linda can not only sing but also dance.
琳達不僅會唱歌，也會跳舞。

Sam went abroad not only to study English but to broaden his horizons as well.
山姆出國不僅是為了學英語，也是為了拓展視野。

Josh is late not only because he overslept but because he missed the bus as well.
喬許遲到不僅是因為他睡過頭，也是因為他錯過了公車。

練習 Exercises

  請選出適當的字詞填入空格中。

Choose the correct word(s) to complete each sentence.

well	polite	not only	pleasure	this

❶ It's a _____ to meet you, Mr. Tanaka.
❷ Jim is not only nice but outgoing as _____.
❸ Students should be _____ to their teachers.
❹ Olivia, _____ is my boss, Daisy.
❺ Melissa plays _____ the piano but also the guitar.

Lesson 38

Self-introduction
自我介紹

實用會話 Dialogue

朗讀 ▶ Lesson 38

🅐 What's your name?

🅑 Brandon. And you are Rachel, right?

🅐 You got it. What do you do for a living, Brandon?

🅑 I'm a web designer.

🅐 No kidding. So am I!

🅐 你叫什麼名字？

🅑 布蘭登。妳是瑞秋，對嗎？

🅐 你說對了。你從事什麼行業，布蘭登？

🅑 我是網站設計師。

🅐 真的假的？我也是耶！

單字片語 Vocabulary and Phrases

❶ You got it.　你說對了。

= You're / That's right.

❷ living [ˈlɪvɪŋ] *n.* 生計

for a living　為了謀生 / 生存

I teach for a living.

我教書維生。

❸ web [wɛb] *n.* 網站 (= website [ˈwɛbˌsaɪt])；網子

❹ designer [dɪˈzaɪnɚ] *n.* 設計師

❺ No kidding.　真的假的？ / 別開玩笑了。(非正式用語)

= For real?

= Really?

Ⓐ Ron is moving to the US.

Ⓑ No kidding. / For real? / Really?

Ⓐ 榮恩要搬去美國了。

Ⓑ 真的假的？ / 別開玩笑了。

口語技能 Speaking Skills

❶ And you are Rachel, right?　妳是瑞秋，對嗎？

◆ 本句句尾的 right [raɪt]，表「對嗎？ / 對不對？」。此種句子稱作附加問句 (或反問句)。

Tom and Mary aren't dating, right?

湯姆與瑪麗沒有交往，對嗎？

John can speak Spanish, right?

約翰會說西班牙語，對嗎？

Helen loves pink, right?

海倫很喜歡粉紅色，對嗎？

2 What do you do for a living, Brandon?
你從事什麼行業，布蘭登？

◆ 詢問職業你可以這樣說：
What do you do for a living?　你從事什麼行業？
What do you do?　你的職業是什麼？

3 So am I!　我也是耶！

◆ 本句使用簡應句，用以表示「……也是 / 也不是」。
　a 若要回應的句子為肯定句，應使用 so 或 too。
　　A I am 16 years old.
　　B So am I. / I am, too.
　　A 我十六歲。
　　B 我也是。

　　A I can play the violin.
　　B So can I. / I can, too.
　　A 我會拉小提琴。
　　B 我也會。

　　A I went to the movies last night.
　　B So did I. / I did, too.
　　A 我昨晚去看了電影。
　　B 我也有去。

b 若要回應的句子為否定句，則使用 neither 或 either。

🅐 I'm not good at basketball.

🅑 Neither am I. / I'm not, either.

🅐 我不擅長打籃球。

🅑 我也不擅長。

🅐 I can't go to the party.

🅑 Neither can I. / I can't, either.

🅐 我無法去派對。

🅑 我也無法。

🅐 I never lie.

🅑 Neither do I. / I don't, either.

🅐 我從不說謊。

🅑 我也不會。

替換看看 Substitution

1 附加問句實用句

And you are Rachel, right?　妳是瑞秋，對嗎？

Eddie is leaving tomorrow, right?　艾迪明天離開，對嗎？

Wendy won first place, right?　溫蒂贏得第一名，對嗎？

2 「你從事什麼行業，布蘭登？」可以怎麼說：

What do you do for a living, Brandon?

What do you do, Brandon?

3 「真的假的？我也是耶！」可以怎麼說：

No kidding. So am I!

No kidding. I am, too!

練習 **Exercises**

請選出適當的字詞填入空格中。

Choose the correct word(s) to complete each sentence.

designer	right	kidding	So	living

1. No _____! I'm from Australia, too.
2. Katrina is a web _____.
3. Jennifer, what do you do for a _____?
4. You're Mr. Samson, _____?
5. You're a doctor? _____ am I!

Lesson 39

Nice to Meet You
很高興認識你

實用會話 Dialogue

朗讀 ▶

Lesson 39

A Nice to meet you. My name is Nicholas.

B Nice to meet you **as well**. I'm Amy.

A Do you come to this **bookstore** often?

B **Actually**, yes. I work here.

A No wonder I always see you here!

A 很高興認識妳。我叫尼可拉斯。

B 我也很高興認識你。我是艾咪。

A 妳常來這間書店嗎？

B 其實，沒錯。我在這裡工作。

A 難怪我常常在這裡看到妳！

單字片語 **Vocabulary and Phrases**

❶ as well　也；還有

Emily will come to the party, and Sam will <u>as well</u>.

= Emily will come to the party, and Sam will, <u>too</u>.

艾蜜莉會來派對，山姆也會。

❷ bookstore [`buk͵stɔr] *n.* 書店

❸ actually [`æktʃʊəlɪ] *adv.* 事實上，其實

= in fact

= as a matter of fact

Emma looks 20, but, <u>actually</u>, she is already 40.

= Emma looks 20, but, <u>in fact</u>, she is already 40.

= Emma looks 20, but, <u>as a matter of fact</u>, she is already 40.

艾瑪看起來像二十歲，但事實上她已經四十歲了。

口語技能 **Speaking Skills**

❶ 頻率副詞

◆ 課文中使用頻率副詞 often（經常）與 always（總是）。下列為常見的頻率副詞，頻率由高至低為：

always [`ɔlwez]	總是（100%）
usually [`juʒʊəlɪ]	通常（80%）
often [`ɔfən]	經常（60%）
sometimes [`sʌm͵taɪmz]	有時（40%）
seldom [`sɛldəm]	鮮少（20%）
never [`nɛvɚ]	從不（0%）

CH 3
溝通與社交

167

2 No wonder I always see you here!　　難怪我常常在這裡看到妳！

No wonder...　　難怪……（置句首作副詞，修飾整句）

wonder [ˈwʌndɚ] *n.* 驚奇

No wonder Mary got a good grade on the test. She cheated!

難怪瑪麗考試拿到很好的成績。她作弊！

The batteries are dead. No wonder the camera doesn't work.

電池沒電了。難怪相機無法用。

替換看看　Substitution

1 「我也很高興認識你。我是艾咪。」可以怎麼說：

> Nice to meet you as well. I'm Amy.
>
> Nice to meet you, too. I'm Amy.

2 頻率副詞實用句

> Do you come to this bookstore often?　　你常來這間書店嗎？
>
> Linda is always happy.　　琳達總是很開心。
>
> Peter never borrows money from his friends.
>
> 彼得從不向朋友借錢。

練習 Exercises

🔑 請選出適當的字詞填入空格中。

Choose the correct word(s) to complete each sentence.

| well | bookstore | wonder | often | actually |

1. I take pleasure in working at a(n) _____.
2. Gina will go out tonight, and her friends will as _____.
3. We all thought Kim is Japanese, but, _____, she's Korean.
4. No _____ you speak English so well!
5. Jared _____ forgets people's names.

At School
在學校

實用會話 Dialogue

朗讀
Lesson 40

🅐 Are you **ready** for the **midterm exam** today?

🅑 Not at all.

🅐 Me, neither.

🅑 Let's **study** together. We still have time!

🅐 Not really… The test starts **in** five minutes!

🅐 今天的期中考試你準備好了嗎？

🅑 根本沒有。

🅐 我也沒有。

🅑 咱們一起讀書吧。我們還有些時間！

🅐 不盡然……。考試五分鐘後開始！

單字片語 Vocabulary and Phrases

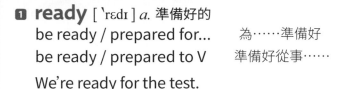

❶ **ready** [`ˋrɛdɪ`] *a.* 準備好的
be ready / prepared for...　　為……準備好
be ready / prepared to V　　準備好從事……

We're ready for the test.
我們已準備好要考試。

I'm ready to meet the challenge.
我已準備好接受挑戰。

❷ **midterm** [`ˋmɪd͵tɝm`] *a.* 期中的 & [`͵mɪdˋtɝm`] *n.* 期中考試
final [`ˋfaɪn!`] *a.* 期末的 & *n.* 期末考試
a midterm / final exam　　期中 / 末考試

❸ **exam** [`ɪgˋzæm`] *n.* 考試
take an exam　　參加考試
pass / fail an exam　　通過 / 沒有通過考試

Evan did well on the exam.
伊凡考試考得很好。

❹ **study** [`ˋstʌdɪ`] *vi.* & *vt.* 學習
（三態為：study, studied [`ˋstʌdɪd`], studied）
study for an exam　　為某個考試讀書
study at + 學校　　在某所學校就讀
study law / business　　攻讀法律 / 商業

Many students are studying in the library.
許多學生正在圖書館讀書。

Judy is now studying at Harvard University.
茱蒂現在就讀哈佛大學。

❺ **in +** 一段時間　　若干時間之後
= 一段時間 + later

Audrey told me that she would be back in an hour.
= Audrey told me that she would be back an hour later.
奧黛莉告訴我她一小時後就會回來。

口語技能　Speaking Skills

❶ "Not at all." 的用法

◆ "Not at all."（一點也不。）用於否定語氣中，特別是當說話者
想要加強否定語氣時。其中片語 at all 表「根本，絲毫，一點」。

not at all 　　一點也不

Ⓐ Do you know how to solve this math problem?

Ⓑ Not at all.

Ⓐ 你知道怎麼解這道數學問題嗎？

Ⓑ 壓根不知道。

比較

not... at all 　　一點也不 / 根本不……

This comedy show is not interesting at all.

這檔喜劇節目一點也不有趣。

Peter does not work hard at all.

彼得一點也不努力。

🔑 Notes

"Not at all." 亦可表「不客氣」，用於禮貌回覆他人的道謝。

Ⓐ Lisa, thanks for your help!

Ⓑ Not at all. / You're welcome.

Ⓐ 麗莎，謝謝妳的幫忙！

Ⓑ 不客氣。

❷ "Not really." 的用法

◆ "Not really."（不盡然 / 不完全。）用於否定語氣中，惟語氣較委婉，其
意思相當於 "Not exactly."，例句如下：

Ⓐ You like singing, don't you?

Ⓑ No, not really / exactly.

Ⓐ 你喜歡唱歌，對嗎？

Ⓑ 不完全如此。

替換看看 Substitution

1 「今天的期中 / 期末考試你準備好了嗎？」可以怎麼說：

> Are you ready for the midterm / final (exam) today?
>
> Are you prepared for the midterm / final (exam) today?

2 「今天的期中考試你準備好了嗎？」可以怎麼說：

> Are you ready for the midterm exam today?
>
> Are you ready to take the midterm exam today?

3 「不盡然。」可以怎麼說：

> Not really.
>
> Not exactly.

CH
3

溝通與社交

練習 Exercises

 請選出適當的字詞填入空格中。

Choose the correct word(s) to complete each sentence.

ready	midterm	all	study	in

❶ The concert starts _____ 10 minutes.

❷ I need to _____ for the finals.

❸ How did you do on your _____ exam.

❹ Are you _____ for the surprise?

❺ The comedian is not funny at _____ .

解答 ❶ in ❷ study ❸ midterm ❹ ready ❺ all

Lesson 41

When Is the Assignment Due?
作業什麼時候要交呢？

實用會話 Dialogue

朗讀 ▶
Lesson 41

A Mr. Todesca!

B Yes, Beverly?

A When is this assignment due?

B It's due next class.

A OK. Are we allowed to work on it with a partner?

B No. This is a personal essay. You should write it alone.

A 陶德斯卡老師！

B 貝芙麗，怎麼了？

A 這份作業什麼時候要交呢？

B 下一堂課要交。

A 好的。我們可以和一位搭檔一起完成嗎？

B 不行。這是個人的短文。妳應該獨自完成。

單字片語 Vocabulary and Phrases

❶ **assignment** [əˋsaɪnmənt] *n.* 作業；分派任務

❷ **allow** [əˋlaʊ] *vt.* 允許，讓
allow sb to V　　允許某人從事……
Visitors aren't allowed to feed the animals in the zoo.
遊客不可以餵食動物園裡的動物。

❸ **work on + N/V-ing**　　(著手) 進行……，從事……
Cole is busy working on a project now.
柯爾現在忙於進行一項計畫。

❹ **partner** [ˋpɑrtnɚ] *n.* 搭檔，夥伴

❺ **personal** [ˋpɝsn̩l] *a.* 個人的，私人的
personal belongings　　個人隨身攜帶物品

❻ **essay** [ˋɛse] *n.* 短文；論文；散文
write / do an essay　　寫論文 / 文章

❼ **alone** [əˋlon] *adv.* & *a.* 單獨地 / 的

口語技能 Speaking Skills

❶ You should write it alone.　　妳應該獨自完成。

　ⓐ 句中的 should 為助動詞，其後須接原形動詞，should 表「一種義務」，譯成「應該」，意思等同於 ought to。
　You should go to work on time.
= You ought to go to work on time.
　你應該準時上班。

　ⓑ 句中的 alone 為副詞，表「單獨地」，亦可作形容詞，表「單獨的，獨自的」，意思等同於 by oneself、on one's own，惟後兩者較常於日常口語中使用。

Chloe enjoys being <u>alone</u> on weekends.
= Chloe enjoys being <u>by herself</u> on weekends.
= Chloe enjoys being <u>on her own</u> on weekends.
克蘿伊享受在週末時與自己獨處。

替換看看 Substitution

❶ 「你應該獨自完成。」可以怎麼說：

> You should / ought to write it alone.
>
> You should / ought to write it by yourself.
>
> You should / ought to write it on your own.

練習 Exercises

請選出適當的字詞填入空格中。

Choose the correct word(s) to complete each sentence.

on	assignment	alone	allowed	partner

❶ Jim was assigned to be my _____.

❷ Ivy has been working _____ this project for two weeks.

❸ I have an English _____ to do.

❹ Customers are not _____ to enter this room.

❺ I prefer to do the experiment _____.

 ❺ alone ❹ allowed ❸ assignment ❷ on ❶ partner 解答

177

Lesson 42

At Work
上班

實用會話 Dialogue

朗讀 ▶

Lesson 42

🅐 In today's **meeting**, we will talk about how to be more **efficient** than before. Does anybody have any ideas?

🅑 Maybe we should **stop checking** Instagram so much while we are working.

🅐 What? Who does that?

🅑 Not me, of course!

🅐 我們將在今天的會議上討論如何比以前更有效率。有人有任何想法嗎？

🅑 或許我們該停止在上班時查看 Instagram。

🅐 什麼？是誰這麼做？

🅑 當然不是我！

單字片語 Vocabulary and Phrases

❶ meeting [ˋmitɪŋ] *n.* 會議

❷ efficient [ɪˋfɪʃənt] *a.* 有效率的

比較

effective [ɪˋfɛktɪv] *a.* 有效的

❸ stop + V-ing　　停止做……

My sister stopped crying soon after she saw Dad come in.

我妹妹看到爸爸走進來時便不再哭了。

比較

stop to V　　停下目前的事去做……

My sister stopped to laugh when Dad hugged her.

爸爸擁抱我妹妹時,她停下活動開始笑起來。

❹ check [tʃɛk] *vt. & vi.* 檢查;核對

Check the product carefully before you buy it.

仔細檢查商品後再購買。

CH
3
溝通與社交

口語技能 Speaking Skills

❶ 一般比較級

◆ 本文中的 more efficient(比較有效率的)是形容詞 efficient 的比較級。
一般會用比較級來比較兩者間程度、級別上的不同。形容詞、副詞的比
較級變化如下:

ⓐ 原級是單音節或大多數雙音節的形容詞或副詞,在字尾
加 -er,如:

smart(聰明的)　　→　　smarter(比較聰明的)

cold(冷的)　　→　　colder(比較冷的)

tall(高的)　　→　　taller(比較高的)

fast(快地 / 的)　　→　　faster(比較快地 / 的)

Notes

在口語會話中，有些雙音節的形容詞或副詞之比較級可在其前加上 more，亦可在字尾加 –er，如下：

friendly（友善的）	→	more friendly（比較友善的） friendlier
quiet（安靜的）	→	more quiet（比較安靜的） quieter
gentle（溫柔的）	→	more gentle（比較溫柔的） gentler

b 少數原級是雙音節的單字以及三音節以上的形容詞或副詞會在其前加上 more，如：

expensive（昂貴的）	→	more expensive（比較貴的）
beautiful（漂亮的）	→	more beautiful（比較漂亮的）
fluently（流利地）	→	more fluently（比較流利地）

c 原級是以子音結尾的單音節形容詞變成比較級時，要先重複該子音字尾，再加 -er，如：

hot（熱的）	→	hotter（比較熱的）
fat（胖的）	→	fatter（比較胖的）

d 有些單字的比較級採不規則變化，如：

good（好的）	→	better（比較好的）
bad（壞的）	→	worse（比較壞的）

替換看看 Substitution

1 「我們將討論如何比以前更有效率。」可以怎麼說：

We will talk about how to be more efficient than before.

We will discuss how to be more efficient than before.

2 「有人有任何想法嗎？」可以怎麼說：

> Does anybody have any ideas?
> ―――――――――――――――――――――
> Does anyone have any ideas?

練習 Exercises

🔑 請選出適當的字詞填入空格中。

Choose the correct word(s) to complete each sentence.

meeting	more	stop	efficient	check

1 The workers need to be _____ polite to customers.

2 The _____ was postponed due to bad weather.

3 Sam sure can get the job done. He is highly _____.

4 Please _____ the document before you send it.

5 When will the baby _____ crying?

CH 3 溝通與社交

Lesson 43

Employee of the Year
年度最佳員工

實用會話 Dialogue

朗讀 ▶
Lesson 43

Ⓐ Katy, you are the winner of the award for "employee of the year!" Congratulations!

Ⓑ Wow, what an honor! Thank you so much!

Ⓐ Also, I have a question: Can you work overtime today? We are busier than usual.

Ⓑ Um, I guess so…

Ⓐ 凱蒂,妳是「年度最佳員工」的得獎者!恭喜妳!

Ⓑ 哇,真榮幸啊!謝謝你!

Ⓐ 我還有一個問題:妳今天可以加班嗎?我們比平常還要忙。

Ⓑ 呃,應該可以吧……。

182

單字片語 Vocabulary and Phrases

❶ winner [`wɪnɚ] *n.* 獲勝者

❷ award [ə`wɔrd] *n.* 獎；獎賞；獎品
an / the award for... ⋯⋯的獎項

❸ employee [ɪm`plɔɪi] *n.* 員工，僱員

❹ congratulations [kənˌgrætʃə`leʃənz] *n.* 恭喜，祝賀 (恆用複數)
Congratulations on your success!
恭喜你成功了！

❺ honor [`ɑnɚ] *n.* 榮幸，光榮
a great honor 莫大的榮幸

❻ work overtime 加班工作
overtime [`ovɚˌtaɪm] *adv.* & *n.* 加班時間

❼ busy [`bɪzɪ] *a.* 忙碌的

❽ usual [`juʒʊəl] *a.* 平常的，慣例的
as usual 照常，照例

口語技能 Speaking Skills

❶ 感歎句簡化

◆ 以 What 起首的感歎句的簡化規則如下：
What + 名詞 + 主詞 + be 動詞 / 一般動詞!
→ What + 名詞!

◆ 根據上述，本課句子可還原為：
What an honor! 真榮幸啊！(簡化說法)
→ What an honor this award is!
　　　　　　　　　主詞　　be 動詞
這個獎項真榮幸啊！

◆ 其他常見以 What 起首的簡化感歎句：
What a surprise!　　真驚喜啊！
What a coincidence!　　真巧啊！
What a day!　　真漫長（的一天）啊！/ 真開心（的一天）啊！
What a shame / pity!　　真可惜啊！

2 I guess so...　　應該可以吧……。

◆ 副詞 so 可代替肯定的 that 子句，若為 not 則是代替否定的 that 子句。

A Do we have a choice?

B I guess so. (so = that we have a choice)
　　I guess not. (not = that we don't have a choice)

A 我們有得選擇嗎？

B 應該有吧。
　　應該沒有。

◆ 根據上述，本課句子可改寫如下：
I guess so...　　應該可以吧……。
= I guess that I can work overtime today...
我今天應該可以加班。

替換看看 Substitution

1 「恭喜（你贏得這項獎）！」可以怎麼說：

Congratulations (on winning the award)!

2「真榮幸 / 驚喜 / 巧 / 漫長的一天 / 可惜啊！」可以怎麼說：

> What an honor!
>
> What a surprise!
>
> What a coincidence!
>
> What a day!
>
> What a shame / pity!

3「呃，應該可以 / 不能吧……。」可以怎麼說：

> Um, I guess so...
>
> Um, I guess not...

練習 Exercises

請選出適當的字詞填入空格中。

Choose the correct word(s) to complete each sentence.

> busy　　employee　　honor　　What　　overtime

1 _____ a surprise! I didn't expect John to show up.

2 There is a new _____ at the office.

3 I'm helping Anna because she is too _____ .

4 We should earn extra money when we work _____ .

5 It's a great _____ to be here!

Lesson 44

Bless You
保重

實用會話 Dialogue

朗讀 ▶
Lesson 44

🅐 Achoo!

🅑 Bless you. Are you getting sick?

🅐 Yes. I am going to see the doctor after work. Achoo!

🅑 Maybe you should go now...

🅐 But then I won't be able to attend the meeting.

🅑 Sure, but if you go to the meeting, you will make us all sick!

🅐 哈啾！

🅑 保重。你生病了嗎？

🅐 是的。我下班後要去看醫生。
哈啾！

🅑 或許你現在就該去……。

🅐 但這麼一來我就無法參加會議了。

🅑 沒錯，但如果你來參加會議，你會害大家都生病！

單字片語 **Vocabulary and Phrases**

1 bless [blεs] *vt.* 祝福；保佑
blessing [`blεsɪŋ] *n.* 祝福；保佑(可數)
be blessed with... 享有……之福
a blessing in disguise 塞翁失馬，焉知非福；因禍得福(諺語)

Jim is blessed with a good sense of humor.
吉姆受到老天眷顧，天生就有幽默感。

John was injured in a car accident, but the nurse that took care of him in the hospital became his girlfriend. That's really a blessing in disguise.
約翰在車禍中受傷了，但在醫院照顧他的護理師卻成了他女友。真是因禍得福。

* disguise [dɪs`gaɪz] *n.* 偽裝

2 sick [sɪk] *a.* 生病的，不舒服的；噁心想吐的
get sick 生病 (= feel ill)
be sick 嘔吐
feel sick 反胃，噁心

3 doctor [`dɑktɚ] *n.* 醫生
the doctor's (clinic) 診所
see / visit the doctor 看醫生
= go to the doctor's

4 be able to V 有能力做……
= be capable of + V-ing

Albert is able to do the presentation on his own.
= Albert is capable of doing the presentation on his own.
艾伯特可以自己做報告。

5 attend [ə`tɛnd] *vt. & vi.* 參加，出席
Several actors and actresses will attend the ceremony.
有幾位男、女演員會出席這場典禮。

CH
3
溝通與社交

口語技能 Speaking Skills

1 Bless you. 保重。

◆ 聽到別人打噴嚏時，你可以這樣說：
Bless you! 保重！

◆ 其用意是希望打噴嚏者能好好保重。此句原為：
May God bless you! 願上帝賜福於你！

◆ 除此之外，若要感謝他人的協助，亦可用 "Bless you!" 回應，此時表「願上帝保佑你（們）！」如：
A Let me help you with your luggage.
B Oh, bless you.
A 讓我來幫你拿行李吧。
B 喔，願上帝保佑你。

2 表達生病的說法

◆ 口語會話中常用下列字詞來表達生病或身體不舒服：
get sick 生病
feel ill 生病（較正式）
feel unwell 不舒服（較正式）
feel / be under the weather 生病 / 不舒服
feel off-color 不舒服

替換看看 Substitution

1 「你生病了嗎？」可以怎麼說：

Are you getting sick?

Are you feeling ill?

Are you feeling unwell?

Are you feeling under the weather?

Are you feeling off-color?

2 「我下班後要去看醫生。」可以怎麼說：

> I am going to see / visit the doctor after work.
>
> I am going to go to the doctor's after work.

3 「但這麼一來我就無法參加會議了。」可以怎麼說：

> But then I won't be able to attend the meeting.
>
> But then I won't be capable of attending the meeting.

練習　Exercises

 請選出適當的字詞填入空格中。

Choose the correct word(s) to complete each sentence.

able	sick	attend	Bless	doctor

1 Jane, are you getting _____ ?

2 Harry was not feeling well so he went to see the _____ .

3 _____ you! Do you need a tissue?

4 More than 100 people will _____ the event.

5 I won't be _____ to go to the meeting tonight.

Choosing a Present
挑選禮物

實用會話 Dialogue

朗讀 ▶
Lesson 45

🅐 Are you going to Tina's birthday party?

🅑 Yes, but I don't know what gift to buy for her.

🅐 I think chocolates are the best idea. She really loves them.

🅑 Yes, but they are the most obvious choice. Everybody will buy them.

🅐 你會去蒂娜的生日派對嗎？

🅑 會，可是我不知道要買什麼禮物送她。

🅐 我想巧克力是最棒的主意。她很喜歡巧克力。

🅑 對，可是巧克力是最顯而易見的選項。大家都會買它們。

單字片語 Vocabulary and Phrases

❶ gift [gɪft] *n.* 禮物
= present [ˈprɛzṇt]

❷ buy [baɪ] *vi. & vt.* 買（三態為：buy, bought [bɔt], bought）
　　buy sth for sb　　買某物給某人
= buy sb sth

　　I would like to buy a doll for my younger sister.
= I would like to buy my younger sister a doll.
　　我想買一個娃娃給我妹妹。

❸ chocolate [ˈtʃɑk(ə)lɪt] *n.* 巧克力

❹ obvious [ˈɑbvɪəs] *a.* 明顯的

　　It is obvious that Sam is lying.
　　很明顯山姆在說謊。

❺ choice [tʃɔɪs] *n.* 選擇
　　make a choice　　做出選擇

　　It's hard to make a choice between cake and ice cream.
　　很難在蛋糕跟冰淇淋之間做出選擇。

❻ everybody [ˈɛvrɪˌbɑdɪ] *pron.* 每個人
= everyone [ˈɛvrɪˌwʌn]

　　At the end of the concert, everybody stood up.
= At the end of the concert, everyone stood up.
　　演唱會結束時，大家都站起來了。

CH
3
溝通與社交

191

 口語技能 Speaking Skills

1 最高級的形態及用法

◆ 本課的 best（最好的）及 most obvious（最顯而易見的）皆為最高級形容
詞。最高級是由形容詞或副詞變化而成，表示「最……」。

a 一般而言，形容詞或副詞的最高級變化有下列原則：

1 大多數雙音節或三音節以上的形容詞或副詞只須在前加最高級
副詞 most，修飾該形容詞或副詞。

beautiful　美麗的　→　most beautiful
clearly　清楚地　　→　most clearly

2 形容詞或副詞若為單音節，則須在字尾加上 -est。

tall　高的　　　　　→　tallest
fast　快速的 / 地　→　fastest

3 形容詞或副詞字尾若為 e，變成最高級時應刪去 e、加 -est。

wise　聰明的　　　→　wisest
cute　可愛的　　　→　cutest

4 形容詞或副詞字尾若為 y，變成最高級時應刪去 y、加 -iest。

pretty　漂亮的　　→　prettiest
easy　容易的 / 地　→　easiest

5 若形容詞或副詞的字尾為「子音 + 母音 + 子音」的組合時，字尾
的子音字母須重複一次，再加上 -est，以形成最高級。

big　大的　　　　　→　biggest
hot　熱的；燙的　　→　hottest

b 大多數的形容詞或副詞會依循以上的規則變化，但仍有些形容詞或
副詞的最高級為不規則變化。

good　好的　　　　→　best
well　好　　　　　　→　best
bad　壞的；糟的　　→　worst
badly　差　　　　　→　worst
many / much　多的　→　most
little　小的；少的　→　least

c 若要表示「最不……」，則要在形容詞或副詞前加上副詞 least。

pretty　漂亮的　　　→　least pretty

favorite　最喜歡的　→　least favorite

替換看看 Substitution

1 最高級的實用句

They are the most <u>obvious</u> choice.　巧克力是最顯而易見的選項。

Mark received the <u>highest</u> grade on the test.
馬克這份考試拿到最高的成績。

The festival is the <u>biggest</u> one of the year.
這個節慶是今年最盛大的。

2 「大家都會買它們。」可以怎麼說：

Everybody will buy them.

Everyone will buy them.

練習 Exercises

 請選出適當的字詞填入空格中。

Choose the correct word(s) to complete each sentence.

most	choice	best	obvious	Everybody

① This is the _____ place in town to try dumplings.

② _____ took part in the project so we finished it early.

③ Sally was forced to make a(n) _____ between the two boys.

④ Which shop sells the _____ expensive chocolates?

⑤ It is _____ that the kids will love the toys.

Chapter 4

休閒娛樂 Leisure Activities

Lesson 46

How Romantic!
真浪漫啊！

實用會話 Dialogue

A Aww! How **romantic**!

B You mean how **boring**?

A This **movie's** not boring!

B The **couple** always gets back together.

A I know. But it's still very sweet!

B I'm going to get more popcorn.

A 噢！真浪漫啊！

B 你是說真無聊？

A 這部電影才不無聊！

B 情侶最後總會復合。

A 我知道。但還是很甜蜜！

B 我要去多拿點爆米花。

單字片語 Vocabulary and Phrases

❶ romantic [roˈmæntɪk] *a.* 浪漫的

The romantic young man bought his wife some roses.

那位浪漫的年輕人買了些玫瑰花給他老婆。

❷ boring [ˈbɔrɪŋ] *a.* 無聊的，乏味的

This book is boring, so I'd like to read another one.

這本書很無聊，所以我想看別本。

❸ movie [ˈmuvɪ] *n.* 電影

= film [fɪlm]

the movies　　電影院

= the movie theater

= the cinema [ˈsɪnəmə]（英式用法）

❹ couple [ˈkʌpl̩] *n.* 一對情侶 / 夫妻

🔑 Notes

couple 可視作單數名詞，亦可視作複數名詞，若想強調的是「一對」則該名詞可視為單數，若想強調的是「男方」及「女方」兩個分別的人則可視為複數名詞。

❺ popcorn [ˈpɑpˌkɔrn] *n.* 爆米花（不可數）

CH
4
休閒娛樂

口語技能 Speaking Skills

❶ 感歎句簡化

◆ 以 How 起首的感歎句的簡化規則如下：

How + 形容詞 / 副詞 + 主詞 + be 動詞 / 一般動詞!

→ How + 形容詞 / 副詞!

◆ 根據上述，本課句子可還原為：

How romantic! 真浪漫啊！（簡化說法）

→ How romantic the movie is!

　　　　主詞　　be 動詞

這部電影真浪漫啊！

You mean how boring? 你是說真無聊？（簡化說法）

→ You mean how boring the movie is?

　　　　　　主詞　　be 動詞

你是說這部電影真無聊？

2 I'm going to get more popcorn. 我要去多拿點爆米花。

◆ 此句的時態為簡單未來式，表示「將來發生的動作或狀態」，簡單未來式的形式及用法如下：

be going to + 原形動詞 + 未來的時間（口語會話常用）

= will + 原形動詞 + 將來的時間

Lucy is going to buy some groceries this afternoon.

= Lucy will buy some groceries this afternoon.

露西今天下午要去買一些食品雜貨。

替換看看 Substitution

1「（這部電影）真浪漫啊！」可以怎麼說：

How romantic!

How romantic the movie is!

2「我要去多拿點爆米花。」可以怎麼說：

I am going to get more popcorn.

I will get more popcorn.

練習 Exercises

請選出適當的字詞填入空格中。

Choose the correct word(s) to complete each sentence.

How	romantic	popcorn	couple	going

1. Actually, many men also like _____ movies.
2. Jane is _____ to get movie tickets for us.
3. The _____ decided to watch a horror movie.
4. _____ boring! I slept through the entire movie.
5. Craig always eats _____ during a movie.

CH
4
休閒娛樂

Watching Movies
看電影

實用會話 Dialogue

朗讀 ▶
Lesson 47

Ⓐ Do you want to go to the movies this Saturday?

Ⓑ That **depends**. Is anything good playing at the theater?

Ⓐ Yes. There's a new **horror** film called *Zombie Children*.

Ⓑ No way!

Ⓐ 這週六你想去看電影嗎？

Ⓑ 看情況。電影院現在有什麼好看的電影上映嗎？

Ⓐ 有的。有一部新的恐怖片叫《殭屍小孩》。

Ⓑ 我才不看！

單字片語 **Vocabulary and Phrases**

❶ depend [dɪˋpɛnd] *vi.* 視⋯⋯而定
　 depend on... 　　視⋯⋯而定，取決於⋯⋯

　 Ⓐ Are you coming hiking this weekend?
　 Ⓑ That / It depends. I've got a lot of work to finish.
　 Ⓐ 這個週末你要跟我們一起去遠足嗎？
　 Ⓑ 那得看情況。我有很多工作得完成。

　 Your entrance into university depends on your exam scores.
　 你的大學入學許可要視考試成績而定。

❷ play [ple] *vi.* (電影) 上映
　 That movie will play at the cinema soon.
　 那部電影即將在電影院上映。

❸ theater [ˋθiətɚ] *n.* 電影院 (= cinema [ˋsɪnəmə])；劇院

❹ horror [ˋhɔrɚ] *n.* 恐怖，恐懼
　 a horror movie / film 　　恐怖片
　 To one's horror,... 　　嚇壞某人的是，⋯⋯

　 To my horror, I realized a thief was in my house.
　 嚇壞我的是，我發現家裡有小偷。

❺ zombie [ˋzɑmbɪ] *n.* 殭屍

❻ children [ˋtʃɪldrən] *n.* 小孩 (複數)
　 child [tʃaɪld] *n.* 小孩 (單數)

口語技能 **Speaking Skills**

❶ 看電影用語

　 ◆ 表「看電影」，你可以這樣說：
　　 go to the movies 　　看電影 (movies 恆為複數)
　　 Chris often goes to the movies
　　 on weekends.
　　 克里斯週末時常去看電影。

◆ 若表「看一場電影」，你可以這樣說：

watch / see a movie　　看一場電影

= go to a movie

= go see / catch a movie

2 電影種類的說法

action	動作片	fantasy	奇幻片
adventure	冒險片	horror	恐怖片
animation	動畫片	romance	愛情片
comedy	喜劇片	thriller	驚悚片
documentary	紀錄片	science fiction	科幻片
drama	戲劇片	(= sci-fi [ˋsaɪˏfaɪ])	

3 "No way!" 的用法

◆ "No way!"（絕不！/ 門兒都沒有！）於口語中使用時，用以表示強烈否定對方的說法、提議等。

Ⓐ Let's go take the roller coaster!

Ⓑ No way!

Ⓐ 我們去搭雲霄飛車吧！

Ⓑ 門兒都沒有！

🔑 **Notes**

當聽到某件令人驚訝、不敢置信的事時，亦可使用 "No way!" 回覆，此時意思為「不可能！」，等於 "Impossible!"。

Ⓐ Tracy, I won the lottery!

Ⓑ No way! You've got to be kidding me!

Ⓐ 崔西，我中樂透了！

Ⓑ 不可能！你在跟我開玩笑吧！

替換看看 Substitution

❶ 「這週六你想去看（場）電影嗎？」可以怎麼說：

> Do you want to go to the movies this Saturday?
>
> Do you want to watch / see a movie this Saturday?
>
> Do you want to go to a movie this Saturday?
>
> Do you want to go see / catch a movie this Saturday?

❷ 「電影院現在有什麼好看的電影上映嗎？」可以怎麼說：

> Is anything good playing at the theater?
>
> Is anything good playing at the movie theater?
>
> Is anything good playing at the movies?
>
> Is anything good playing at the cinema?

練習 Exercises

🖊 請選出適當的字詞填入空格中。

Choose the correct word(s) to complete each sentence.

play	horror	depends	way	theater

❶ I'm not in the mood for a _____ movie.

❷ When will this film _____ at the cinema?

❸ No _____ ! I will not go on a date with Eric.

❹ All the movies at the _____ are new this week.

❺ It's not too much to say that my future _____ on this test.

解答 ❶ horror ❷ play ❸ way ❹ theater ❺ depends

I Never Lose!
我從來沒輸過！

實用會話 Dialogue

朗讀 ▶
Lesson 48

Ⓐ Hey, do you want to go shoot some hoops?

Ⓑ Sure! Where should we go?

Ⓐ The basketball court at Green Park is usually free.

Ⓑ Are you ready to lose again?

Ⓐ I never lose!

Ⓐ 嘿，你想要去打籃球嗎？

Ⓑ 好啊！我們該去哪裡呢？

Ⓐ 葛林公園的籃球場通常空著沒人使用。

Ⓑ 你準備好再輸一場了嗎？

Ⓐ 我從來沒輸過！

單字片語 Vocabulary and Phrases

❶ shoot [ʃut] *vt.* & *vi.* 投 / 射 (球)；射擊；拍攝 (影片)
（三態為：shoot, shot [ʃɑt], shot）
　　shoot (some) hoops　　打籃球（非正式用語）
= 　shoot (some) baskets （非正式用語）
= 　play basketball
　　shoot an arrow　　射箭
　　shoot a movie / film　　拍電影

Aim at the target before you shoot.
瞄準好了再射擊。

That movie studio is currently shooting a movie in my hometown.
那家製片廠現在正在我的老家拍電影。

❷ hoop [hup] *n.* 籃框；環
❸ basketball [ˋbæskɪtˏbɔl] *n.* 籃球
　　a basketball player / coach / team　　籃球球員 / 教練 / 球隊

📌 **Notes**

說明從事某運動時，不須在球類名詞前方置定冠詞 the，如：
play basketball / baseball / volleyball　　打籃球 / 棒球 / 排球
但表示演奏樂器時，則須在樂器名詞前方置定冠詞 the，如：
play the flute / the piano / the drums　　吹笛子 / 彈鋼琴 / 打鼓

❹ court [kɔrt] *n.* 球場
　　a basketball / tennis / badminton court　　籃球 / 網球 / 羽球場
❺ free [fri] *a.* 不在使用的；免費的
　　for free　　免費地
　　a free gift / ticket　　免費的禮物 / 票券

Is this seat free?
這是個空位嗎？

CH 4 休閒娛樂

❻ **lose** [luz] *vi.* & *vt.* 輸掉 (比賽) (三態為：lose, lost [lɔst], lost)
win [wɪn] *vi.* & *vt.* 贏得 (比賽) (三態為：win, won [wʌn], won)

Our school's baseball team lost / won the game.
我們學校的棒球隊輸 / 贏了比賽。

口語技能 Speaking Skills

❶ 「go + 動詞原形」的用法

◆ 本課會話中的 "Do you want to go shoot some hoops?" (你想要去打籃球嗎？) 於動詞 go 後面直接置原形動詞，這是在日常美語常見的用法，表「去做某事」，動詞 come 亦常見此種用法。

go / come + 原形動詞　　去做……
Let's go take the train.
我們去搭火車吧。
Kelly, come visit me if you're in town!
凱莉，如果妳到城裡，就來看看我吧！

❷ 籃球場相關用詞

basketball court 籃球場
backboard 籃板
three-point line 三分線
hoop 球框
free throw lane 罰球圈
net 籃網
free throw line　罰球線

替換看看　Substitution

❶ 「你想要去打籃球嗎？」可以怎麼說：

> Do you want to go shoot (some) hoops?
>
> Do you want to go shoot (some) baskets?
>
> Do you want to go play basketball?

練習　Exercises

請選出適當的字詞填入空格中。

Choose the correct word(s) to complete each sentence.

free	basketball	hoop	lost	shoot

❶ Annie was upset because she _____ the game.

❷ Excuse me. Is this seat _____ ?

❸ Let's go _____ some baskets!

❹ Carol shot the ball, but missed the _____ .

❺ The team usually practices _____ after school.

解答　❶ lost　❷ free　❸ shoot　❹ hoop　❺ basketball

Playing Basketball
打籃球

實用會話 Dialogue

朗讀 ▶ Lesson 49

Ⓐ There's no way you can make that three-point shot.

Ⓑ Watch me.

Ⓐ Wow! Right in the hoop.

Ⓑ Now do you want to see me slam-dunk?

Ⓐ You are such a show-off.

Ⓐ 你不可能投進那顆三分球的。

Ⓑ 看著吧。

Ⓐ 哇！空心入籃。

Ⓑ 那你想要看我灌籃嗎？

Ⓐ 你真是個愛現的人。

單字片語 **Vocabulary and Phrases**

❶ shot [ʃɑt] *n.* 投 / 射 / 擊球
make a shot　　投球
a three-point shot　　三分球
Good shot!　　好球！

❷ watch [wɑtʃ] *vt.* & *vi.* 看
We killed time by watching TV.
我們看電視來打發時間。

❸ right [raɪt] *adv.* 正好，恰好
Right here / there.　　就在這 / 那裡。

❹ slam-dunk [ˈslæmdʌŋk] *vi.* & *vt.* 灌籃
a slam dunk　　灌籃
slam [slæm] *n.* 砰的一聲
dunk [dʌŋk] *n.* & *vi.* & *vt.* 灌籃

❺ show-off [ˈʃoˌɔf] *n.* 喜歡賣弄的人；愛炫耀的人
show off　　賣弄；炫耀

Robert just wants to show off his new house to us.
羅伯特只是想要向我們炫耀他的新房子。

口語技能 **Speaking Skills**

❶ There's no way you can make that three-point shot.
你不可能投進那顆三分球的。

There is no way + that 子句（that 可省略）
……是不可能的
= There is no way of + N/V-ing
= There is no way to V
= It is impossible to V

CH 4 休閒娛樂

There is no way (that) we can win the game.
= There is no way of winning the game.
= There is no way to win the game.
= It is impossible for us to win the game.
我們不可能贏得這場比賽的。

2 such 的用法

◆ 本課會話中的 "You are such a show-off."（你真是個愛現的人。）有限
定詞 such，表「如此，這麼」，其用法如下：
such + a / an +（形容詞）+ 單數可數名詞
Mr. Harrison is such a nice person.
哈里森先生真是個好人。
such + 不可數名詞 / 複數可數名詞
The company provided us with such professional service.
這間公司提供給我們相當專業的服務。

3 籃球術語

shoot the ball	投籃 (= make a shot)
dunk	灌籃 (= slam dunk)
jump shot	跳投
dribble	運球
three pointer	三分球 (= three-point shot)
point guard	控球後衛
shooting guard	得分後衛
power forward	大前鋒
small forward	小前鋒
center	中鋒

替換看看 Substitution

1 「你不可能投進那顆三分球的。」可以怎麼說：

> There's no way (that) you can make that three-point shot.
>
> There's no way of making that three-point shot.
>
> There's no way to make that three-point shot.
>
> It's impossible for you to make that three-point shot.

2 「丹尼投了一顆三分球。」可以怎麼說：

> Danny made a three-point shot.
>
> Danny made a three pointer.

3 「那你想要看我灌籃嗎？」可以怎麼說：

> Now do you want to see me slam dunk?
>
> Now do you want to see me do a slam dunk?
>
> Now do you want to see me do a dunk?

CH
4

休閒娛樂

練習 **Exercises**

請選出適當的字詞填入空格中。

Choose the correct word(s) to complete each sentence.

right	shot	such	show-off	way

❶ There's no _____ we will be on time for the game.

❷ The millionaire is _____ a humble person.

❸ Don't be a poor winner. Nobody likes a _____ .

❹ It was amazing when Zack made that three-point _____ .

❺ Please put the chair _____ there.

Lesson 50

At the Mall
在購物商場

實用會話 Dialogue

朗讀 ▶
Lesson 50

A I want to go into this store for a second.

B Really only one second?

A OK, maybe a few minutes. I need a new purse.

B What's wrong with that one?

A It's so old and too small!

B OK, fine. Let's go in.

A 我想要進去這間店一下子。

B 真的只有一下子嗎？

A 好吧，可能幾分鐘。
我需要新的手提包。

B 妳手上的那個哪裡不好了？

A 它又舊又小！

B 好吧。咱們進去吧。

單字片語 Vocabulary and Phrases

❶ store [stɔr] *n.* 商店

❷ second [ˈsɛkənd] *n.* 秒
Just a second.　稍等片刻。
= Just a sec [sɛk].

❸ purse [pɝs] *n.* 手提包（美式用法）
= handbag [ˈhændˌbæg]（英式用法）

> 🔑 **Notes**
>
> 在英式用法中，purse 是指小錢包，等同於美式用法中的 wallet [ˈwɑlɪt]。

❹ What's wrong with sth/sb?　某物 / 某人怎麼了？
= What's the matter with sth/sb?
= What's the problem with sth/sb?
What's wrong with Jamie?
詹米怎麼了？

❺ old [old] *a.* 舊的；老的

口語技能 Speaking Skills

❶ 副詞 maybe 的用法

maybe [ˈmebi / ˈmebɪ] *adv.* 也許，可能
= perhaps [pɚˈhæps]
　ⓐ maybe 使用時應置句首。
　　John maybe can join us next time. (✕)
　→ Maybe John can join us next time. (○)
　= Perhaps John can join us next time.
　　約翰下次可能可以加入我們。

　ⓑ maybe 不同於 may be。maybe 為副詞，而 may be 是在 be 動詞之前加了助動詞 may，常譯為「也許是」。

May be you are right.（✕）
→ Maybe you are right.（○）
也許你是對的。

You maybe right.（✕）
→ You may be right.（○）
你也許是對的。

❷ What's wrong with that one?　妳手上的那個哪裡不好了？

◆ 口語會話中經常利用代名詞 one 或 ones 來代替重複出現的可數名詞或名詞片語。one 可以用來代替先前提過的單數名詞；ones 則可以用來代替先前提過的複數名詞。

Robin doesn't like his old cell phone; he wants a new cell phone.（劣）
→ Robin doesn't like his old cell phone; he wants a new one.（佳）
羅賓不喜歡他的舊手機；他想要一支新的。

◆ 根據上述，本句句尾的 one 即指前一句提到的 purse（手提包），因此本句原為：

What's wrong with that purse?
你手上的那個手提包哪裡不好了？

◆ 但因為 purse 上一句已出現過，為了避免內容重複宜以代名詞 one 代替，而形成本句：

What's wrong with that one?
你手上的那個哪裡不好了？

替換看看 Substitution

❶「我需要新的手提包。」可以怎麼說：

I need a new purse.

I need a new handbag.

2 「你手上的那個哪裡不好了？」可以怎麼說：

> What's wrong with that one?
>
> What's the matter with that one?
>
> What's the problem with that one?

3 「好吧，可能幾分鐘。」可以怎麼說：

> OK, maybe a few minutes.
>
> OK, perhaps a few minutes.

練習　Exercises

請選出適當的字詞填入空格中。

Choose the correct word(s) to complete each sentence.

purse	ones	Maybe	one	second

1 I don't like these sweaters, but those _____ look nice!

2 Please stop the car for a(n) _____ .

3 Roger got his girlfriend a fancy _____ for her birthday.

4 _____ we should eat at home.

5 Jerry bought a new hat, so he threw away his old _____ .

Lesson 51

In the Fitting Room
在試衣間

實用會話 Dialogue

朗讀
Lesson 51

A Can I please try these **pants** on?

B Sure. The **fitting room** is over there.

A Thanks.

B So how are they?

A They are too small. Can you **get** me some bigger ones?

B Sure. One size bigger?

A Maybe three **sizes** bigger!

A 我可以試穿褲子嗎？

B 當然。試衣間在那邊。

A 謝謝。

B 所以褲子如何？

A 太小了。你可以幫我拿
一些更大的嗎？

B 當然。大一個尺寸嗎？

A 可能要大三個尺寸！

單字片語 Vocabulary and Phrases

❶ pants [pænts] *n.* 長褲（因褲管有兩條，故恆用複數）
a pair of pants　一件長褲

🔑 **Notes**

下列單字亦使用類似用法：
shorts [ʃɔrts] *n.* 短褲
jeans [dʒinz] *n.* 牛仔褲
trousers [ˈtrauzɚz] *n.* 長褲
leggings [ˈlɛgɪŋz] *n.* 緊身褲

❷ fitting room　試衣間
❸ get sb sth　幫某人拿某物
= get sth for sb
Could you please get me a piece of paper?
= Could you please get a piece of paper for me?
可以麻煩你幫我拿一張紙嗎？

❹ size [saɪz] *n.* 尺寸，大小

口語技能 Speaking Skills

❶ Can I please try these pants on?　我可以試穿褲子嗎？

try sth on / try on sth　試穿／戴某衣物
try [traɪ] *vt.* 試用；嘗試
I would like to try these shoes on.
我想試穿這雙鞋子。
I'm sorry; you can't try on the underwear.
很抱歉；你不能試穿內衣。

比較

try sth out / try out sth 　　試用 / 試驗某物

You should try out the product before you buy it.

你應該在購買前先試用產品。

替換看看　Substitution

❶ 「我可以試穿褲子 / 短褲 / 牛仔褲 / 長褲 / 緊身褲嗎？」可以怎麼說：

Can I please try these pants on?

Can I please try these shorts on?

Can I please try these jeans on?

Can I please try these trousers on?

Can I please try these leggings on?

❷ 「你可以幫我拿一些更大的嗎？」可以怎麼說：

Can you get me some bigger ones?

Can you get some bigger ones for me?

練習 Exercises

請選出適當的字詞填入空格中。

Choose the correct word(s) to complete each sentence.

fitting	try	size	pants	got

❶ Andy _____ Sandy a bouquet of flowers for their date.

❷ How much is this pair of _____?

❸ Where is the _____ room?

❹ I need one _____ smaller, please.

❺ The customer wants to _____ on this dress.

 解答　❶ got　❷ pants　❸ fitting　❹ size　❺ try

Lesson 52

Getting a Discount
打折

實用會話 Dialogue

朗讀
▶
Lesson 52

🅐 Hi, can I get a discount on this perfume? It's a present for Mother's Day.

🅑 Sorry, the lowest price I can give you is $50.

🅐 Hmm... I think I will try somewhere else.

🅑 Actually, we have the cheapest deal in town for this perfume.

🅐 嗨，這瓶香水我可以有優惠嗎？這是母親節要送的禮。

🅑 抱歉，我能開的最低價格是五十美元。

🅐 嗯……。我想我會去別間店看看。

🅑 其實，這瓶香水我們的價格是城裡最便宜的。

CH
4

休閒娛樂

221

單字片語 Vocabulary and Phrases

❶ perfume [`pɝfjum] *n.* 香水 (不可數)
a bottle of perfume　一瓶香水

❷ present [`prɛzn̩t] *n.* 禮物

❸ Mother's Day　母親節
Father's Day　父親節

❹ price [praɪs] *n.* 價格，價錢

❺ cheap [tʃip] *a.* 便宜的
expensive [ɪk`spɛnsɪv] *a.* 昂貴的

❻ deal [dil] *n.* 交易 & *vi.* 交易；處理 (三態為：deal, dealt [dɛlt], dealt)
deal in...　從事……的買賣
deal with...　處理……

Nathan deals in used cars.
納森從事中古車買賣。

Melissa is dealing with the situation right now.
梅莉莎現在正在處理該問題。

口語技能 Speaking Skills

❶ discount 的用法

discount [`dɪskaʊnt] *n.* 折扣
get a discount on sth　就某物得到折扣
give sb a... discount on sth　就某物給某人打……折
= give sb... off on sth
You can get a discount on this bag if you pay with a credit card.
如果您用信用卡付費，您購買這個包包可以獲得折扣。
They gave me a 20% discount on the suit.
= They gave me 20% off on the suit.
這套西裝他們給我打八折。

📌 Notes

中文與英文對於表達打折的說法相反。

10% off	打九折	60% off	打四折
20% off	打八折	70% off	打三折
30% off	打七折	80% off	打兩折
40% off	打六折	90% off	打一折
50% off	打五折		

discount 亦可作及物動詞：

discount [dɪsˋkaʊnt] *vt.* 打折

Stores discount most things around holidays.

商店在假期前後會減價大部分商品。

替換看看 Substitution

❶ 「這瓶香水我可以有優惠嗎 / 你可以給我優惠嗎？」可以怎麼說：

> Can I get a discount on this perfume?
> Can you give me a discount on this perfume?

❷ 「這是母親節 / 父親節要送的禮。」可以怎麼說：

> It's a present for Mother's Day / Father's Day.
> It's a gift for Mother's Day / Father's Day.

223

練習 Exercises

請選出適當的字詞填入空格中。

Choose the correct word(s) to complete each sentence.

deal	present	price	perfume	discount

❶ What is the _____ of this computer?

❷ Mr. O'Brien asked for a _____ on the car.

❸ Did you buy a birthday _____ for Kelly?

❹ This _____ has a fruity smell to it.

❺ The store has the best _____ in town for cameras.

解答 ❶ price ❷ discount ❸ present ❹ perfume ❺ deal

At the Party
在派對上

實用會話 Dialogue

朗讀 ▶ Lesson 53

🅐 This **cocktail** is delicious, Adam. What's in it?

🅑 **Pineapple** juice, **coconut** milk, and **rum**.

🅐 It goes well with this fruit **salad**. Good idea!

🅑 Thanks. Next you should try some **wine** and cheese.

🅐 I will! Great music, also. Who is this?

🅑 It's my friend's **band**. I'll **invite** you next time they play a **concert**!

CH 4 休閒娛樂

🅐 這雞尾酒很好喝，亞當。
裡面有什麼？

🅑 鳳梨汁、椰奶跟蘭姆酒。

🅐 這跟水果沙拉搭配起來很
好。好點子！

🅑 謝謝。你接下來應該試試
看一些葡萄酒跟起司。

🅐 我會的！而且，音樂很棒。
這位歌手是誰？

🅑 這是我朋友的樂團。下次
他們辦演唱會我會邀請你來！

單字片語 Vocabulary and Phrases

❶ **cocktail** [ˈkɑkˌtel] *n.* 雞尾酒

❷ **pineapple** [ˈpaɪnˌæpḷ] *n.* 鳳梨

❸ **coconut** [ˈkokənət] *n.* 椰子

❹ **rum** [rʌm] *n.* 蘭姆酒

❺ **salad** [ˈsæləd] *n.* 沙拉

❻ **wine** [waɪn] *n.* 葡萄酒
　　red / white wine 　紅酒 / 白酒

❼ **band** [bænd] *n.* 樂團

❽ **invite** [ɪnˈvaɪt] *vt.* 邀請
　　I wasn't invited to the party.
　　我沒有被邀請去派對。

❾ **concert** [ˈkɑnsɚt] *n.* 演唱會；音樂會

口語技能 Speaking Skills

❶ It goes well with this fruit salad. 　這跟水果沙拉搭配起來很好。

A go with B 　A 與 B 相配
Do you think this necklace goes with my dress?
你覺得這條項鍊搭配我的洋裝好看嗎？

❷ 簡略句型

◆ 若可明確知道說話者所指的事物為何，在非正式的口語會話中英美人士
經常將代名詞與 be 動詞予以省略，形成較簡短的句型。
Look! There is a dog.
= Look! A dog.
你看！(有) 一隻狗。

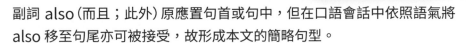

◆ 根據上述，本課之簡略句 "Great music, also."
（而且，音樂很棒。）可還原為：

Also, this is great music.

副詞 also（而且；此外）原應置句首或句中，但在口語會話中依照語氣將 also 移至句尾亦可被接受，故形成本文的簡略句型。

❸ "Who is this?" 與 "Who is it?" 的用法

◆ 本課句子 "Who is this?"（這位歌手是誰？）中的指示代名詞 this 即 指 this singer（這位歌手）。此處的 this 亦可換成代名詞 it。"Who is this?" 與 "Who is it?" 亦可用於下列情境：

ⓐ 打電話時：

🅐 Who is this?

🅑 This is John. / It's John.

🅐 請問是誰？

🅑 我是約翰。

ⓑ 在屋內聽到門外有人敲門時：

🅐 Who is it?

🅑 It's Vicky.

🅐 請問是誰？

🅑 我是薇琪。

🔑 **Notes**

以上兩個情境在詢問對方是誰時，因為雙方並非面對面見面，不宜使用 "Who are you?"。回答時，亦不應說 "I'm John." 或 "I'm Vicky."

CH 4

休閒娛樂

替換看看 Substitution

1 "A go with B" 的實用句

> It goes well with this fruit salad. 這跟水果沙拉搭配起來很好。
>
> Red wine goes particularly well with steak.
> 紅酒與牛排搭配起來特別合適。
>
> Your shoes really go with your pants. 你的鞋子跟褲子很搭。

2 「這位（歌手）是誰？」可以怎麼說：

> Who is this?
> Who is it?

練習 Exercises

請選出適當的字詞填入空格中。

Choose the correct word(s) to complete each sentence.

concert	invite	band	with	cocktail

1 I would like to _____ you to my birthday party.

2 That hat goes well _____ your shirt!

3 You must be at least 18 to order a(n) _____ .

4 Simon and his friends went to a(n) _____ last night.

5 Jim started a(n) _____ with some of his friends.

Thank You for Coming
謝謝你前來

實用會話 Dialogue

朗讀

Lesson 54

A Thanks for having me over, Nancy. That was a great party!

B Thank you for coming. It was really fun!

A Sorry that I broke your living room table.

B It's fine. Accidents happen.

A Next time I will host a party!

B I can't wait for it!

A 謝謝妳邀請我來，南希。
那真是很棒的派對！

B 謝謝你前來。真的很好玩！

A 很抱歉我弄壞了妳客廳的桌子。

B 沒關係。意外難免會發生。

A 下次我來主辦派對！

B 我等不及了！

CH
4
休閒娛樂

單字片語 Vocabulary and Phrases

❶ party [ˋpɑrtɪ] *n.* 派對

❷ break [brek] *vt.* 弄壞，損壞
(三態為：break, broke [brok], broken [ˋbrokən])

Sammy broke his ankle and was sent to the hospital.
山米的腳踝骨折被送到醫院了。

❸ living room　　客廳

❹ It's fine.　　沒關係。
= It's OK.
= Don't worry about it.　　別放在心上。

❺ host [host] *vt.* 主辦；主持
host a party　　主辦派對

口語技能 Speaking Skills

❶ Thanks for having me over, Nancy.　　謝謝妳邀請我來，南希。

have sb over　　邀請某人來自己家
= invite sb over
I'm having a couple of friends over for dinner.
= I'm inviting a couple of friends over for dinner.
我邀請一些朋友來我家吃晚餐。

❷ Accidents happen.　　意外難免會發生。

= Accidents will happen.

◆ 此說法在口語會話中較為常見，常用於回應某人因他所造成的意外而道歉。
accident [ˋæksədənt] *n.* 意外；事故
比較
an accident waiting to happen　　勢必會發生的意外；早晚會出事

The bridge needs maintenance. It's just an accident waiting to happen.

這座橋需要維修。這裡早晚會出事的。

❸ I can't wait for it!　我等不及了！

can't wait for sth / to V　等不及某事 / 做⋯⋯

I can't wait for the movie to premiere.

我等不及電影首映了。

Jenny can't wait to go on the trip.

珍妮等不及要去那趟旅程了。

替換看看　Substitution

❶「謝謝妳邀請我來，南希。」可以怎麼說：

> Thanks for having me over, Nancy.
>
> Thanks for inviting me over, Nancy.

❷「沒關係 / 別放在心上。意外難免會發生。」可以怎麼說：

> It's fine. Accidents happen.
>
> It's OK. Accidents happen.
>
> Don't worry about it. Accidents happen.

練習 **Exercises**

 請選出適當的字詞填入空格中。

Choose the correct word(s) to complete each sentence.

host	broke	over	wait	Accidents

❶ Don't worry about the broken glass. _____ happen.

❷ Dylan can't _____ to celebrate his birthday.

❸ Luke _____ his mom's vase with a baseball.

❹ Jocelyn had her friends _____ for dinner.

❺ Do you want to _____ a surprise party for Jake?

Traveling Abroad
出國旅遊

實用會話 Dialogue

朗讀 ▶
Lesson 55

Ⓐ What should we do for the long **weekend**?

Ⓑ How about a **trip** to Japan? I want to go **skiing**!

Ⓐ That sounds cold and tiring. Let's go shopping in Korea.

Ⓑ How about this: Let's take **separate** trips!

Ⓐ Great idea!

Ⓐ 我們連假應該要做什麼呢？

Ⓑ 去日本旅遊如何？我想去滑雪！

Ⓐ 聽起來又冷又累。咱們去韓國購物吧。

Ⓑ 這樣如何：咱們就各自旅遊吧！

Ⓐ 好主意！

CH
4
休閒娛樂

233

單字片語 Vocabulary and Phrases

❶ **weekend** [ˈwikˌɛnd] *n.* 週末
weekday [ˈwikˌde] *n.* 平日，工作日
on weekends　　在週末
on weekdays　　在平日

❷ **trip** [trɪp] *n.* 旅遊
a business trip　　出差

Did you enjoy your trip to France?
你去法國的行程好玩嗎？

❸ **ski** [ski] *vi.* 滑雪 & *n.* 滑雪板（常用複數）
a pair of skis　　一副滑雪板

❹ **separate** [ˈsɛp(ə)rɪt] *a.* 分開的，不同的 & [ˈsɛpəˌret] *vt.* 使分開；區分
separate A from B　　把 A 與 B 區分開

My sister and I sleep in separate rooms.
我姊姊與我睡在不同的房間。

I was separated from my friends when we went to college.
我和我的朋友上大學後就分開了。

口語技能 Speaking Skills

❶ 「go + 現在分詞」的用法

◆ 本文的句子 "I want to go skiing!"（我想去滑雪！）中的 go skiing（去滑雪）採用「go + 現在分詞」的用法，表示「從事某種休閒活動」。現在分詞即為「動詞 + ing」。並非所有動詞的現在分詞都適合採用此用法。一般情況下，該用法僅適合休閒、有娛樂性質的活動，如下：
go hiking　　　　去健行
go swimming　　去游泳
go jogging　　　去慢跑
go camping　　　去露營
go golfing　　　去打高爾夫球

go snorkeling [ˈsnɔrklɪŋ]　去浮潛

go shopping　去購物

I go hiking with my brother on weekends.

我週末都與我哥哥去健行。

Henry likes to go jogging by himself.

亨利喜歡自己一個人去慢跑。

Would you like to go shopping with me?

你想要跟我一起去購物嗎？

2 表示「好主意」的說法

◆ 要表示「好主意！」，你可以這樣說：

Great idea!

That's a good idea!

That sounds like a good idea!

Sounds like a good idea!

Sounds great!

替換看看　Substitution

1 「我想去滑雪 / 健行 / 游泳 / 慢跑 / 露營 / 打高爾夫球 / 浮潛 / 購物！」可以怎麼說：

I want to go skiing!

I want to go hiking!

I want to go swimming!

I want to go jogging!

I want to go camping!

I want to go golfing!

I want to go snorkeling!

I want to go shopping!

CH
4

休閒娛樂

練習 Exercises

請選出適當的字詞填入空格中。

Choose the correct word(s) to complete each sentence.

idea	weekend	skiing	separate	trip

1. My boss went on a business _____ to Canada.
2. The family plans to go _____ in Japan for the holidays.
3. Kelly's parents sleep in _____ bedrooms.
4. I'd love to go camping. That's a good _____!
5. What should we do for the _____?

Planning a Trip
規劃旅遊

實用會話 Dialogue

朗讀 ▶ Lesson 56

A We should book our **flights** today.

B Yes! There's a flight that **departs** in the morning.

A Sounds great!

B We should also make a reservation at the **resort** soon.

A Look at this one. It has a queen-sized bed and **balcony**.

B Oh, no! It's **already** booked!

A 我們應該今天訂機票。

B 好!有一班飛機在早上出發。

A 好主意!

B 我們也應該儘快預訂度假飯店。

A 瞧瞧這個。它有加大雙人床和陽臺。

B 喔,不!它已經被訂走了!

CH
4
休閒娛樂

單字片語 Vocabulary and Phrases

❶ flight [flaɪt] *n.* 班機；飛行
What time does your flight arrive?
你的班機幾點抵達？

❷ depart [dɪˋpɑrt] *vi.* 出發；離開
depart for + 地方　　出發前往某地

The train for Boston departs at 8 o'clock every morning.
前往波士頓的火車每天早上八點發車。

Mr. Lee will depart for Singapore tomorrow.
李先生明天將前往新加坡。

❸ resort [rɪˋzɔrt] *n.* 度假飯店，度假勝地
a summer resort　　避暑勝地

❹ balcony [ˋbælkənɪ] *n.* 陽臺

❺ already [ɔlˋrɛdɪ] *adv.* 已經
Hurry up! We're already late for the meeting.
快一點！我們開會已經遲到了。

口語技能 Speaking Skills

❶ 表示「預訂」的說法

book [bʊk] *vt. & vi.* 預訂（房間、座位、門票等）
= reserve [rɪˋzɝv]
I would like to book a room for two nights.
= I would like to reserve a room for two nights.
我想訂一間房間住兩個晚上。

🔖 Notes

book 之後亦可接「人」作受詞，表示「為某人預訂……」。
My secretary booked me a flight to Canada next week.
我的祕書幫我預訂下週去加拿大的班機。

表示「預訂」也可以說：

make a reservation for... 預訂……

reservation [ˌrɛzɚˈveʃən] *n.* 預訂

I would like to book a room for two nights.

= I would like to make a reservation for a room for two nights.

2 各種床型大小的說法

single [ˈsɪŋgl̩] *a.* 單人的
double [ˈdʌbl̩] *a.* 雙人的
queen-sized [ˈkwinsaɪzd] *a.* 加大的 (= queen-size)
king-sized [ˈkɪŋsaɪzd] *a.* 特大的 (= king-size)

a	single	bed	單人床
	double		雙人床
	queen-sized		加大雙人床
	king-sized		特大雙人床

🔑 Notes

表示「房型大小」時，有下列常見的說法：

a single (bed) room / a single　　單人房

a double (bed) room / a double　（有一張雙人床的）雙人房

a twin (beds) room　（有兩張單人床的）雙人房

a queen-size (bed) room / a queen room

（有一張加大雙人床的）雙人房

a king-size (bed) room / a king room

（有一張特大雙人床的）雙人房

替換看看 Substitution

❶ 「我們應該今天訂機票。」可以怎麼說：

> We should book our flights today.
>
> We should reserve our flights today.

❷ 「我們也應該儘快預訂度假飯店的房間。」可以怎麼說：

> We should also make a reservation for a room at the resort soon.
>
> We should also book a room at the resort soon.
>
> We should also reserve a room at the resort soon.

❸ 「它有加大雙人床 / 特大雙人床 / 雙人床 / 單人床和陽臺。」可以怎麼說：

> It has a queen-sized bed and balcony.
>
> It has a king-sized bed and balcony.
>
> It has a double bed and balcony.
>
> It has a single bed and balcony.

練習 Exercises

請選出適當的字詞填入空格中。

Choose the correct word(s) to complete each sentence.

depart	book	resort	reservation	flight

1. The _____ is scheduled to leave at 1:30 p.m.
2. We'll be staying at a summer _____ for vacation.
3. Jenny called the hotel to make a _____ .
4. Which hotel did you _____ for our trip?
5. The plane will _____ at 9:45 a.m.

Checking In
櫃檯報到

實用會話 Dialogue

朗讀 ▶
Lesson 57

A Is that your carry-on bag?

B Yes, it is.

A Please put it on the scale. Oh! That is too heavy. You need to check it in.

B Can I take out some things and add them to my check-in luggage?

A No, your check-in luggage is already at the limit!

A 這是您的隨身行李嗎？

B 是的。

A 請您放到秤上。喔！那太重了。
您必須將它托運。

B 我可以把一些東西拿出來放進我
的托運行李嗎？

A 不行，您的托運行李已經達到重
量上限了！

Chanunphat / Shutterstock.com

單字片語 Vocabulary and Phrases

❶ scale [skel] *n.* 秤，磅秤 (= scales)

❷ heavy [`hɛvɪ] *a.* 重的
light [laɪt] *a.* 輕的

❸ take out sth / take sth out 取出某物
John took out his notebook and wrote something down.
約翰把他的筆記本拿出來並寫下一些東西。

❹ add A to B 將 A 加到 B 上
add [æd] *vt.* & *vi.* 增加，添加
Fiona added some spices to her soup.
費歐娜在她的湯裡加了一些香料。

❺ limit [`lɪmɪt] *n.* 極限，上限；界限
be at the limit 達到上限
= reach the limit
within limits 有限度地
I can help you, but within limits.
我可以幫助你，可是只能有限度地。

CH
4
休
閒
娛
樂

口語技能 Speaking Skills

❶ carry-on 與 check-in 的用法

ⓐ carry-on [`kærɪ͵ɑn] *a.* 隨身攜帶的
a carry-on bag 一件隨身行李
carry-on luggage / baggage 隨身行李
Please put your carry-on bag on the table.
請將您的隨身行李放在桌上。

b check-in [ˈtʃɛkˌɪn] *a.* 托運的 & *n.* (機場) 報到；報到櫃檯

check-in luggage / baggage　　托運行李

check-in counter　　報到櫃檯

How much does my check-in luggage weigh?

我的托運行李有多重呢？

Where is the check-in counter?

報到櫃檯在哪裡？

c check in　　(機場) 辦理登機手續；(飯店) 辦理住房手續

We can't check in until 2 o'clock.

我們兩點鐘才能辦理登機手續 / 住房手續。

d check sth in / check in sth　　將某物托運

Will you be checking in any luggage?

您要托運任何行李嗎？

2 名詞 luggage 與 baggage

luggage [ˈlʌgɪdʒ] *n.* 行李 (不可數)

= baggage [ˈbægɪdʒ] *n.* 行李 (不可數)

🔑 Notes

luggage 與 baggage 皆為不可數名詞，不可說：

a luggage / baggage（×）

two luggages / baggages（×）

應說：

a piece of luggage / baggage（○）

two pieces of luggage / baggage（○）

How many pieces of luggage / baggage do you have with you?

您攜帶多少件行李？

替換看看 Substitution

1 「那是您的隨身行李 / 托運行李嗎？」可以怎麼說：

> Is that your carry-on bag?
>
> Is that your check-in luggage?
>
> Is that your check-in baggage?

2 「您的托運行李已經達到重量上限了！」可以怎麼說：

> Your check-in luggage is already at the limit!
>
> Your check-in luggage has already reached the limit!

練習 Exercises

請選出適當的字詞填入空格中。

Choose the correct word(s) to complete each sentence.

> luggage   scale   added   limit   check-in

1 Excuse me. I can't find the _____ counter.

2 The chef _____ some pepper to the dish.

3 The weight _____ for each item is 5 kg.

4 How many pieces of _____ will you take to China?

5 Please put your backpack on the _____ so I can weigh it.

CH 4 休閒娛樂

Lesson 58

At the Airport
在機場

實用會話 Dialogue

朗讀 ▶
Lesson 58

A Could I see your **passport**, please?

B Here you are.

A How long will you be in the US?

B Two weeks.

A And what is the purpose of your visit?

B I want to become a famous **Hollywood actor**.

A I see... Do you have a working **visa**?

B No...

A 不好意思，我可以看你的護照嗎？

B 給你。

A 你會在美國待多久？

B 兩週。

A 你來訪的目的是什麼呢？

B 我想成為知名的好萊塢演員。

A 了解⋯⋯。你有工作簽證嗎？

B 沒有⋯⋯。

單字片語 Vocabulary and Phrases

1 **passport** [`pæs,pɔrt] *n.* 護照

2 **Hollywood** [`halɪ,wud] *n.* 好萊塢

3 **actor** [`æktɚ] *n.* (男) 演員
   actress [`æktrɪs] *n.* 女演員

4 **visa** [`vizə] *n.* 簽證
   a working visa　　工作簽證
   a student visa　　學生簽證
   a tourist visa　　觀光簽證

口語技能 Speaking Skills

1 Could I see your passport, please?　　不好意思，我可以看你的護照嗎？

= May I see your passport, please?

◆ 若要向他人客氣地要求某事物時，可以用下列句型：
Could I..., please?　　不好意思，我可以……嗎？
= May I..., please?
Could I have your name, please?
可以請您把大名給我嗎？
May I have your attention, please?
可以請您注意我這邊嗎？

2 入境審查時的常見問答

◆ 在機場經過入境審查時，審查員通常會詢問來訪該國的目的，即會說：
What is the purpose of your visit?　　你來訪的目的是什麼？
＊ purpose [`pɝpəs] *n.* 目的
　 visit [`vɪzɪt] *n.* 拜訪；參觀

Are you here for business or pleasure?

= For business or pleasure?

你來出差還是旅遊？

＊business [`bɪznɪs] *n.* 商務，公事 (不可數)

　　pleasure [`plɛʒɚ] *n.* 快樂 (不可數)

◆ 針對上列問句，可回覆：

I'm here for business. / For business. 　我來出差的。

I'm here for vacation. / For vacation. 　我來度假的。

I'm here for college. / For college. 　我來就讀大學。

I'm here to visit my family. 　我來探望我家人。

替換看看 Substitution

1 「我想成為知名的好萊塢 (男) 演員 / 女演員。」可以怎麼說：

I want to become a famous Hollywood actor.

I want to become a famous Hollywood actress.

2 「你有工作簽證 / 學生簽證 / 觀光簽證嗎？」可以怎麼說：

Do you have a working visa?

Do you have a student visa?

Do you have a tourist visa?

練習 Exercises

請選出適當的字詞填入空格中。

Choose the correct word(s) to complete each sentence.

May	passport	actor	visa	purpose

1. What is the _____ of your trip to Macau?
2. We traveled to London on a tourist _____ .
3. Please show your _____ when you get on the airplane.
4. _____ I have your phone number, please?
5. Sam's father used to be a famous _____ .

CH 4

休閒娛樂

解答 ① purpose ② visa ③ passport ④ May ⑤ actor

Lesson 59
At the Hotel
在飯店

實用會話 Dialogue

朗讀 ▶
Lesson 59

🅐 This is our hotel, isn't it?

🅑 Yup!

🅐 Wow, you really chose a fancy one, didn't you?

🅑 Only the best for you, my love.

🅐 Look at this lobby. How beautiful! I feel like a princess on her honeymoon. By the way, how much are we paying for this place?

🅑 Please don't ask.

🅐 這是我們要住的飯店，對不對？

🅑 對！

🅐 哇，你真的找了間豪華的飯店，對不對？

🅑 只給妳最好的，親愛的。

🅐 瞧瞧這個大廳。真美啊！我好像個公主在度蜜月。對了，這房間我們要付多少錢啊？

🅑 拜託不要問。

單字片語 **Vocabulary and Phrases**

1 **hotel** [ho`tɛl] *n.* 飯店

2 **choose** [tʃuz] *vt.* & *vi.* 選擇
（三態為：choose, chose [tʃoz], chosen [`tʃozn̩]）

Nancy chose to quit her job.
南希決定要辭職。

3 **fancy** [`fænsɪ] *a.* 昂貴的，豪華的

4 **my love** 親愛的
= my dear

5 **lobby** [`lɑbɪ] *n.* 大廳

6 **princess** [`prɪnsəs] *n.* 公主
prince [prɪns] *n.* 王子

7 **honeymoon** [`hʌnɪˌmun] *n.* 蜜月
go on sb's honeymoon 某人去度蜜月

Taylor is taking the week off to go on her honeymoon.
泰勒這週請假去度蜜月了。

8 **pay** [pe] *vi.* & *vt.* 付（錢）（三態為：pay, paid [ped], paid）
pay for sth 付錢買某物

Victor paid for the meal.
這一餐維克多請客了。

口語技能 **Speaking Skills**

1 This is our hotel, isn't it? 這是我們要住的飯店，對不對？

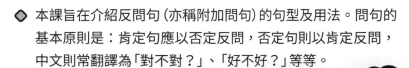

◆ 本課旨在介紹反問句（亦稱附加問句）的句型及用法。問句的
基本原則是：肯定句應以否定反問，否定句則以肯定反問，
中文則常翻譯為「對不對？」、「好不好？」等等。

◆ 肯定句：

John is a nice young man, isn't he?
約翰是位有禮貌的年輕人，對不對？

Kevin will call me, won't he?
凱文會打電話給我，對不對？

You get up early, don't you?
你很早起床，對不對？

Come sit with us, won't you?
你來跟我們一起坐，好不好？

（以原形動詞為首的祈使句，語氣若為邀請、建議，其反問句通常使用
won't you）

Let's take a break, shall we?
咱們休息一下吧，好不好？

（以 let's 引導的祈使句，其反問一律使用 shall we）

◆ 否定句：

You aren't sick, are you?
你沒生病，對不對？

Linda won't come, will she?
琳達不會來，對不對？

Gary didn't come to school, did he?
蓋瑞沒來上學，對不對？

Stop running around, will you?
不要一直跑來跑去，好不好？

（以原形動詞為首的祈使句，語氣若為命令、禁止，其反問句則通常使用
will you）

2 By the way, how much are we paying for this place?
對了，這房間我們要付多少錢啊？

by the way　　順便一提，對了

與他人正在談論某一話題，突然想要改變主題或是突然想到某事時可以說
by the way 或 incidentally [ˌɪnsəˈdɛntḷɪ]。

By the way, Sam called me yesterday.
= Incidentally, Sam called me yesterday.
對了，山姆昨天打電話給我。

There are a lot of handsome boys at that school, incidentally.
= There are a lot of handsome boys at that school, by the way.
順便一提，那所學校有很多英俊的男孩。

替換看看　Substitution

1 反問句的實用句

> Wow, you really chose a fancy one, didn't you?
> 哇，你真的找了間豪華的飯店，對不對？
>
> Andy can finish this by tomorrow, can't he?
> 安迪明天之前會完成這個，對不對？
>
> This is the library, isn't it?　這是圖書館，對不對？

2 「只給妳最好的，親愛的。」可以怎麼說：

> Only the best for you, my love.
>
> Only the best for you, my dear.

CH
4
休
閒
娛
樂

253

練習 **Exercises**

🔖 請選出適當的字詞填入空格中。

Choose the correct word(s) to complete each sentence.

doesn't	fancy	honeymoon	By the way	are

1 The couple is having dinner in a(n) _____ restaurant for their date.

2 We will go on a(n) _____ to Italy after we get married.

3 You aren't going to sleep on the floor, _____ you?

4 Sandra prefers to stay in cheap hotels, _____ she?

5 _____ , where should we go for dinner?

解答 **1** fancy **2** honeymoon **3** are **4** doesn't **5** By the way

Lesson 60

In the Room
在房間內

實用會話 Dialogue

朗讀 ▶ Lesson 60

🅐 It's so **dark** in this **room**. How do we turn on the lights?

🅑 I don't know. I don't see any **switches**.

🅐 Hey, there's a **robot** on the **table**.

🅑 It doesn't **talk**, does it?

🅐 I don't know... Let me try. Robot! Turn on the lights!

🅑 Look at that. The lights are on!

🅐 這房間裡好暗。要怎麼開燈呢？

🅑 我不知道。我沒看到開關。

🅐 嘿，桌子上有一個機器人。

🅑 它不會講話，對不對？

🅐 我不知道……。讓我試試看。機器人！開燈！

🅑 瞧瞧。燈亮了！

255

單字片語 Vocabulary and Phrases

❶ **dark** [dɑrk] *a.* 昏暗的
bright [braɪt] *a.* 明亮的

It's getting dark outside.
外面天色漸暗。

❷ **room** [rum] *n.* 房間

❸ **switch** [swɪtʃ] *n.* (電源) 開關
flip [flɪp] / flick [flɪk] the switch　打開開關

❹ **robot** [`robɑt] *n.* 機器人

❺ **table** [`tebl̩] *n.* 桌子
on the table　在桌上

❻ **talk** [tɔk] *vi.* 說話；談話
talk about...　談論 / 討論⋯⋯
talk to sb　與某人說話

We need to talk about the project.
我們必須討論該計畫。

Helen won't talk to me.
海倫不願意跟我說話。

口語技能 Speaking Skills

❶ It doesn't talk, does it?　它不會講話，對不對？

◆ 之前的課程中介紹過使用 right 的反問句：無論為肯定句或否定句，都可以使用 right 形成反問。
Wendy and Kate are friends, aren't they?
= Wendy and Kate are friends, right?
溫蒂與凱特是朋友，對不對？
You aren't giving up, are you?
= You aren't giving up, right?
你沒有要放棄，對不對？

◆ 根據上述，本課反問句亦可改寫如下：
It doesn't talk, <u>does it</u>?
= It doesn't talk, <u>right</u>?
它不會講話，對不對？

替換看看 Substitution

❶ 「它不會講話，對不對？」可以怎麼說：

> It doesn't talk, does it?
>
> It doesn't talk, right?

練習 Exercises

🔖 請選出適當的字詞填入空格中。

Choose the correct word(s) to complete each sentence.

right	robot	dark	switch	talk

❶ Samuel is training his parrot to _____.
❷ The little boy got a toy _____ for his birthday.
❸ I can't find the _____ for the lights.
❹ Karen is dating James, _____?
❺ It's so _____ in the cave. Let me get my flashlight.

Notes

國家圖書館出版品預行編目（CIP）資料

英語輕鬆學：學好入門會話就靠這本！
／賴世雄作. -- 初版. -- 臺北市：常春藤有聲出版
股份有限公司, 2022.12　面；　公分.
--（常春藤英語輕鬆學系列；E66）
ISBN　978-626-7225-09-7（平裝）
1. CST：英語　2. CST：會話
805.188　　　　　　　　　　　111020264

常春藤英語輕鬆學系列【E66】
英語輕鬆學：學好入門會話就靠這本！

總　編　審	賴世雄
終　　　審	陳宏瑋
執行編輯	許嘉華
編輯小組	鄭筠潔・Nick Roden・Brian Foden
設計組長	王玥琦
封面設計	謝孟珊
排版設計	王穎緁・林桂旭
錄　　音	劉書吟
朗讀播音老師	Terri Pebsworth・Jacob Roth
講解播音老師	奚永慧・Stephen Rong
法律顧問	北辰著作權事務所蕭雄淋律師
出　版　者	常春藤數位出版股份有限公司
地　　　址	臺北市忠孝西路一段 33 號 5 樓
電　　　話	(02) 2331-7600
傳　　　真	(02) 2381-0918
網　　　址	www.ivy.com.tw
電子信箱	service@ivy.com.tw
郵政劃撥	50463568
戶　　　名	常春藤數位出版股份有限公司
定　　　價	399 元

郵票黏貼處

100009 臺北市忠孝西路一段 33 號 5 樓

常春藤有聲出版股份有限公司　行政組　啟

常春藤　www.ivy.com.tw　愛上英語的第一站

讀者問卷【E66】
英語輕鬆學：學好入門會話就靠這本！

感謝您購買本書！為使我們對讀者的服務能夠更加完善，請您詳細填寫本問卷各欄後，寄回本公司或傳真至（02）2381-0918，或掃描 QR Code 填寫線上問卷，我們將於收到後七個工作天內贈送「常春藤網路書城熊贈點 50 點（一點 = 一元，使用期限 90 天）」給您（每書每人限贈一次），也懇請您繼續支持。若有任何疑問，請儘速與客服人員聯絡，客服電話：（02）2331-7600 分機 11～13，謝謝您！

線上填寫
免郵寄最環保

姓　　名：＿＿＿＿＿＿＿＿＿　性別：＿＿＿＿　生日：＿＿＿＿ 年 ＿＿＿ 月 ＿＿＿ 日

聯絡電話：＿＿＿＿＿＿＿＿＿　E-mail：＿＿＿＿＿＿＿＿＿＿＿＿＿

聯絡地址：□□□□□□＿＿＿＿＿＿＿＿＿＿＿＿＿＿＿＿＿＿＿＿＿＿＿
　　　　　＿＿＿＿＿＿＿＿＿＿＿＿＿＿＿＿＿＿＿＿＿＿＿＿＿＿＿＿＿

教育程度：□國小　□國中　□高中　□大專／大學　□研究所含以上
職　　業：**1** □學生
　　　　　2 社會人士：□工　□商　□服務業　□軍警公職　□教職　□其他＿＿＿＿＿

1 您從何處得知本書：□書店　□常春藤網路書城　□FB／IG／Line@ 社群平臺推薦
　　□學校購買　□親友推薦　□常春藤雜誌　□其他＿＿＿＿＿＿＿＿＿＿＿＿＿＿

2 您購得本書的管道：□書店　□常春藤網路書城　□博客來　□其他＿＿＿＿＿＿＿

3 最滿意本書的特點依序是(限定三項)：□試題演練　□字詞解析　□內容　□編排方式
　　□印刷　□音檔朗讀　□封面　□售價　□信任品牌　□其他＿＿＿＿＿＿＿＿＿

4 您對本書建議改進的三點依序是：□無（都很滿意）□試題演練　□字詞解析　□內容
　　□編排方式　□印刷　□音檔朗讀　□封面　□售價　□其他＿＿＿＿＿＿＿＿＿

　　原因：＿＿＿＿＿＿＿＿＿＿＿＿＿＿＿＿＿＿＿＿＿＿＿＿＿＿＿＿＿＿＿＿＿

　　對本書的其他建議：＿＿＿＿＿＿＿＿＿＿＿＿＿＿＿＿＿＿＿＿＿＿＿＿＿＿＿

5 希望我們出版哪些主題的書籍：＿＿＿＿＿＿＿＿＿＿＿＿＿＿＿＿＿＿＿＿＿＿

6 若您發現本書誤植的部分，請告知在：書籍第＿＿＿＿＿＿頁，第＿＿＿＿＿＿行
　　有錯誤的部分是：＿＿＿＿＿＿＿＿＿＿＿＿＿＿＿＿＿＿＿＿＿＿＿＿＿＿＿＿

7 對我們的其他建議：＿＿＿＿＿＿＿＿＿＿＿＿＿＿＿＿＿＿＿＿＿＿＿＿＿＿＿

感謝您寶貴的意見，您的支持是我們的動力！　常春藤網路書城 www.ivy.com.tw